# FIFTY IN REVERSE

# FIFTY IN REVERSE

A NOVEL

BILL FLANAGAN

TILLER PRESS
NEW YORK LONDON TORONTO SYDNEY NEW DELHI

An Imprint of Simon & Schuster, Inc.
1230 Avenue of the Americas
New York, NY 10020



First Tiller Press hardcover edition September 2020



Interior design by Michelle Marchese

Manufactured in the United States of America

1 3 5 7 9 10 8 6 4 2

Library of Congress Cataloging-in-Publication Data

Names: Flanagan, Bill, 1955– author.
Title: Fifty in reverse : a novel / by Bill Flanagan.
Description: First Tiller Press hardcover edition. | New York : Tiller Press, 2020.
Identifiers: LCCN 2020010334 (print) | LCCN 2020010335 (ebook) | ISBN 9781982152673 (hardcover) | ISBN 9781982152697 (ebook)
Subjects: GSAFD: Science fiction.
Classification: LCC PS3556.L313 F54 2020 (print) | LCC PS3556.L313 (ebook) | DDC 813/.54—dc23
LC record available at https://lccn.loc.gov/2020010334
LC ebook record available at https://lccn.loc.gov/2020010335

ISBN 978-1-9821-5267-3
ISBN 978-1-9821-5269-7 (ebook)

*For my son, Frank*

Great thanks to Theresa DiMasi, Sam Ford, Anja Schmidt, Samantha Lubash, Amy Bell, and Max Meltzer, and to Paul Muldoon for the close read.

—Bill Flanagan

# FIFTY IN REVERSE

# ONE

The boy read typed directions to his mother as she drove through a suburb inside Boston's Route 128 halo. They turned right, past the statue of the Minuteman, and parked outside a large white house that was home and office to Dr. Terry Canyon, the motorcycle psychiatrist who had a way with today's troubled teens.

His mother insisted on walking the boy to the door and handing him over. It was tough on her. She believed that bringing her child to a mental health professional was evidence she had failed as a parent. She brought him anyway. Her love was greater than her pride. She shook hands with the doctor's assistant and told the boy she would get some coffee and be back in an hour, waiting right outside. The mother was more nervous than her son.

The boy took a seat in a parlor overfilled with small couches, settees, and hassocks. An antique Spanish guitar was mounted on the wall, along with large color photos of southwestern landscapes and Mexican pyramids. Shelves were crammed with tiny Aztec figurines and Navajo masks, a feathered tambourine, and half a dozen clay pipes. A door slammed and a tall man flew into the room like he was launched from a catapult. He dropped a sheaf of loose papers on one of the couches as he came toward the boy, sticking out his large hand.

"Peter Wyatt! I'm Terry! Terry Canyon! Hey, man—good to meet you!"

The boy offered his hand and was pulled into a hug. Terry Canyon was six feet three inches tall, beefy, with thick blond hair rolling over his collar and ears. He wore a tan jacket that might have been skinned from a deer, blue jeans, and an open neck checked shirt. His belt buckle and ring were turquoise, the color of his eyes. He grinned above a large, dimpled chin. He squeezed the boy, let go of him, laughing, and said, "So they're telling you you're flip city, huh? Sent you to the witch doctor to get your cranium reconfigured. Ouch. I'll tell you who I think is nuts, Pete. These dried-up old conformists with their pie charts and statistics and demographic studies who wouldn't know a moment of uninhibited bliss if it tripped over their wheelchairs. Shit, man. You took off your clothes? So what? Let's outlaw nature, for Christ's sake. Let's write a rule against the human body. I wonder if in fifty years they'll look back and say, 'Those people in 1970 were so insane they covered themselves with pieces of colored cloth even when it was hot outside. Why? Because they were ashamed of their genitals.' How sick is *that*?"

"It's nice of you to say so, Doctor," the boy told him.

"Call me Terry, Pete." He plunged into an overstuffed green couch. He felt through his pockets and came out with a little cigarette—a Tijuana Smalls. "Hey, you smoke?" The boy shook his head no. The doctor lit up. "Good for you. Bad habit. I'm working my way up from Luckys. So—I'm glad you were able to make the trip up here. You freaked out by this whole thing? You shouldn't be. Yossarian, right? *Catch-22.* The only sane response to a crazy world is to act nuts. You feeling okay?"

"Well, Terry, I'm in a pickle."

"Go on, Pete, tell me more."

"I'm under the impression that I went to sleep in the year 2020 as a sixty-five-year-old man and woke up a few days ago, here in April 1970, fifteen years old again. I played along for a while. I enjoyed it. Seeing my parents alive, our old house, my school. But the longer this went on the more anxious I became. Why was I not waking up? Had I had some kind of accident? Have I gone mad?"

Dr. Terry weighed the invitation. He did not speak. The boy looked to be a young fifteen. Tall and gangly with a long neck like someone had grabbed a cute ten-year-old under the ears and yanked him until he stretched.

The boy continued: "Whatever was going on I figured was beyond my control. I'd wait it out. But after three days I thought, I have to get out of here. I need to shock myself out of this dream. I considered jumping off the roof, but that might have gone really wrong. I could have ended up still in 1970 with a broken back. So I took off my clothes in front of the math class. Classic nightmare scenario. I thought it would wake me up. Didn't work."

Dr. Terry mulled this over. "You gave your actions due consideration."

"My options were limited."

"You're from the future."

"That is how it seems to me. If it's a fantasy, it's a detailed and intricate one. You want to know the history of the Red Sox for the next fifty seasons? They win the World Series four times, but not until after the year 2000."

"You're Billy Pilgrim. You've become unstuck in time."

"No, I'm stuck. I want to get home to my wife and children. I want to get home to Starbucks and flat-screen TVs. I miss my iPhone. I'll never complain about the autocorrect function again. I miss Alexa."

"Alexa is your wife?"

"No. My wife is Janice. Alexa turns the lights on."

Dr. Terry got up and walked around the room, exhaling blue cigar smoke. "Look, if I refer to your future life as a delusion, I don't want you to take offense. It's just the terminology we use in the trade."

"Fine with me."

"Great. So listen, let's test this delusion. Okay?"

"Fire away."

"Who are the presidents of the United States from now until your time?"

"Nixon, Ford, Carter, Reagan, Bush one, Clinton, Bush two, Obama, Trump."

"Wait—you're telling me Ronald Reagan becomes president?"

"Two terms—1981 to 1989."

"Pete, he'll be a hundred years old in 1989. Wait, let me get some paper, I should write this down."

The boy went through the list again. The doctor took notes. He said, "Can you tell me the vice presidents?"

"Yeah, let me think. Agnew, Ford, Rockefeller—"

"Nelson Rockefeller?"

"For about two years."

"Shit."

"Agnew gets arrested for taking bribes and Gerald Ford replaces him as Nixon's VP. Then when Nixon resigns . . ."

"Nixon resigns?"

"Under threat of impeachment."

"I love this."

"Ford becomes president and appoints Rockefeller, then Ford is beaten by Jimmy Carter."

"Jimmy?" Dr. Terry was writing as fast as he could.

"Carter's vice president was Mondale. Reagan has George Bush Senior, who succeeds Reagan and picks as his VP Dan Quayle . . ."

"Now you're just making up names."

"Bush and Quayle were followed by Clinton and Gore, who were followed by Bush Junior and Cheney . . ."

"Bush Junior?"

"There are a lot of Bushes. Who are followed by Obama and Biden. Then comes Trump. If I tell you about Trump, you'll have me committed."

Dr. Terry studied his papers. "Right. Okay. Can we do an experiment, Pete?"

"Sure."

"I'm going to jumble up these presidents you gave me and see if you remember them the same way. Cool?"

"Yeah, sure."

For the next ten minutes Dr. Terry asked the boy which president Mr. Gore served under, what years Ford came and went, who succeeded and preceded Clinton—he zigzagged up and down the list trying to throw him off. The boy didn't make any mistakes. He didn't mix up Quayle with Cheney or think that Obama came before Carter. The doctor was impressed with his consistency. He said, "This is a very structured delusion."

"Look, Doctor," the boy told him, "we can do this all day. We can talk the next fifty years of sports, music, TV, world events. Get this—Eastern European communism falls in 1989. The Soviet Union dissolves. Nelson Mandela becomes president of a free and integrated South Africa. All kinds of big stuff happens. President Obama was black."

Dr. Terry walked over to a shelf and studied the bleached skull of a steer. After a minute he declared, "Pete, I'd like to work with you regularly. Two, three sessions a week. How would you feel about that?"

"You're seeing a book in your future . . ."

"I'm seeing a remarkable case study, that's for sure. And listen, man, I studied with Tim Leary at Harvard, okay? I've been on vision quests. I am open to exploring worlds beyond our senses. I say this to you in full honesty: I will take this journey with you wherever it leads us. I admit I'm not convinced you're actually a time traveler from the next century. I'm a doctor, I have to be skeptical of supernatural propositions. But I'm not closing any doors to my own knowledge. If in the course of this expedition you can make it reasonable for me to believe you're from 2020, shit, I'll be pleased and excited. I'm not going to con you, and I trust you won't con me, and we'll see where this road takes us. You in?"

"I can't ask my mother to drive me to Lexington twice a week. We live in Rhode Island."

"One afternoon a week here and I'll come to you Saturday mornings—how's that?"

"Sure, Terry. Be nice to have someone to talk to about all this."

"Solid."

The boy told the doctor, "You can't be my shrink and say *solid*. One or the other."

"Deal." Dr. Terry leaned forward and spoke in a low voice. "Pete—anything we talk about in session is in total confidence. You understand that, yeah?"

"I do."

"Okay, then. Nothing to do with your treatment, but tell me this. Marijuana. 2020. Legal?"

"Some places, Doctor. Massachusetts, Maine, Vermont, Colorado, Illinois, Michigan, Nevada, Alaska, the whole West Coast. It's getting there."

Dr. Terry nodded. Peter spent the rest of the hour describing a world without rabbit ears or milkmen. By the time he got to the extinction of cursive writing and cloth diapers, his mother was outside.

# TWO

As the junior guidance counselor at West Bethlehem Veterans Memorial High School, Maurice Mosspaw was responsible for one-third of the school's 3,200 students. His duties stretched from the morning session, which began at 7:25 a.m., to an hour past the end of the afternoon session at 5:15. Because of overcrowding the school day was staggered. Upperclassmen started early, freshmen stayed late. Moe Mosspaw had school all the time.

Peter Wyatt stripping naked in algebra I was high on Mr. Mosspaw's list of priorities. The Wyatts were a respected and connected family in Bethlehem. The father was a judge. The mother was a teacher's nightmare, the retired head of the Foreign Languages department at Providence College. When her oldest daughter was flunking science back in '65, Joanne Wyatt went through all the science teacher's written comments and sent them back with corrections in substance, grammar, and the proper spelling of the plural *hypotheses.*

When the second Wyatt daughter was going to be dropped from French II, the mother sent the girl to live with a family in

Toulouse for the summer. She came back to school in the fall, conjugating like she was born in the sixth arrondissement.

Any kid losing his mind in the middle of the school day was a problem for Mr. Mosspaw, but Peter Wyatt's breakdown was a special knot of burdens. If it had been a poor kid, a kid with a history of discipline issues—a screwup—they could have shipped the trouble out of the school. But the Wyatts wanted their son reinstated, and they had the money, the connections, and the legal vocabulary to make their case.

Mosspaw was not against it. He barely knew the kid. What he knew very well was that once a fifteen-year-old boy had swung his snorkel at a dozen ninth-grade girls, there were going to be twenty-four angry parents who would not want that boy back in the room with their daughters. Some of them were respected and connected, too.

Vice Principal Alice Lockwood was a tall woman who had served in the Peace Corps in Africa after skipping out on her final vows as a nun. She was a serious person. She had sympathy for a disturbed child, but her first duty was to protect all the other children. She would expect Mr. Mosspaw to handle the Wyatt problem in a way that wouldn't cause more trouble for the school or escalate into anything ugly. The guidance counselor was confident that whatever he did would be wrong.

In the faculty lunchroom he spoke to Mr. Wood, the algebra teacher in whose class Peter Wyatt had unveiled.

"How do you feel about the Wyatt boy coming back tomorrow?"

"Gonna keep his dingaling in his dungarees?"

"You think the other kids will be upset?"

"Upset? I don't think they were upset. I think they were

amused. I think if we left it up to the kids, it would make the yearbook's annual highlights section. I'd be more worried about Wyatt. Shit, Moe, he won't be able to make it out of the locker room without every thug from Oakland Beach slapping the back of his skull and calling him Lady Godiva. Don't worry about the other students. If this poor head case comes back to school, worry about him making it through the week alive."

Mosspaw went back to Vice Principal Lockwood and said that as it was almost the first of May, how about if Peter Wyatt took the rest of the semester off and resumed classes in September? He could study at home for his finals, or he could go to summer school. Ease back in.

The vice principal raised a piece of paper. "This is a note from Dr. Terrence Canyon. Harvard psychiatrist. He strongly recommends that Peter return to class immediately. He needs to start putting this behind him."

Mosspaw said, "Okay, if you think so."

"It's not my decision, Maurice. I don't know the boy. This is your call."

It was settled, then. Whatever happened, Moe Mosspaw would get blamed.

Peter Wyatt returned to algebra I the next day. First period. He walked in with his eyes looking straight ahead and took his place at his desk. He didn't hide from any of the faces staring at him, but he didn't stare back.

Wood came in and pushed a soft leather briefcase across his blotter and looked around with practiced indifference. He said, "Pipe down. Get out your workbooks. Wyatt, you got any surprises planned?"

The class chuckled. Peter stood up from his desk and said, "I want to apologize for the other day, Mr. Wood."

"Don't apologize to me, Peter."

"I want to apologize to the class. I'm very sorry."

His classmates' faces told Peter that his words meant nothing to them. He was still a nonentity who had mutated into a psycho. He was moved to improvise a better story.

"The truth is," he told the class, "I was tripping on acid when I took my clothes off."

It was as if an electrical connection had been switched on under every desk. The kids' mouths formed grins and grimaces and little Os. Wood looked like he was going to execute a flying tackle.

"I didn't know what was happening to me," Peter continued. "I stopped by Lynch's Variety Store before school that day to get some gum and a certain . . . person who no longer goes to this school said, 'Hey, Pete, try *this* gum, it's a new flavor.' I took a stick of what I thought was Beech-Nut and didn't think any more of it until about an hour later when I was sitting in homeroom and saw the bones of my hand and all the veins glowing."

The teacher had missed his shot at a figure-four leglock and had to rotate to Concerned Adult Mode.

"That must have been frightening, Peter. Did you tell your doctor?"

"The doctor told me. I had no idea. I thought I had lost my mind." He watched the reaction from the teacher and the students and then added, "Imagine my relief."

Wood said it was an important lesson to all the students and told Peter to take his seat. The classroom buzzed with low and excited voices until the teacher barked a page assignment and workbooks opened. Math class began its turgid procession.

Peter attempted to focus on the equations. The girl next to him was trying to catch his eye. She had switched places to be near him. Daphne Burrows was the most dangerous girl in ninth grade. She was wearing earrings in the shape of tiny daggers and a choker made of purple ribbon that emphasized her long neck. Peter knew that Daphne delighted in being bad. As she was bright, articulate, and delicately beautiful, her misbehavior faced few impediments. Daphne was a nihilist as well as the only freshman who knew what that word meant and had read the key texts.

Until Peter took off his clothes in class, Daphne never noticed him. When all the kids said he was crazy, it got her interest.

When Daphne had his attention, she laid her left hand, palm up, on the edge of her desk. He watched. She took a tiny art-class razor attached to the end of a metal pencil and ran it down her outstretched forefinger. A red line appeared. She lifted her finger and licked it. She whispered, "I'm crazy too."

Wood asked who knew the reciprocal of negative nine, and Daphne raised the uncut hand. She recited the answer perfectly. Then she said, "Mr. Wood, may I go to the nurse? I'm bleeding."

The class turned to her. She held up her other hand and said, "My finger."

Peter watched her gather her books and leave the room. When she was outside the door she gave him a wink. He understood that his troubles were multiplying.

The story that the kid who took off his clothes in algebra class had been dosed with LSD went around the school as fast as a sneeze. Peter Wyatt became famous as a victim of illegal hallucinogens and a walking warning to parents and teenagers that THIS COULD HAPPEN TO YOU if you didn't keep your eyes open and reject candy from strangers.

The lie worked as a dispensation. Peter was still viewed with suspicion but was officially accepted back into the student body. The price he paid was to be paraded in front of all the school health classes to tell his story.

Lynch's Variety Store suffered condemnation from angry parents for harboring drug-dealing riffraff and was subjected to surprise police inspections for a while, which amounted to officers coming in and having coffee and sniffing through the magazines for subversive material. Lynch's stopped carrying *Ramparts*, and the riffraff moved elsewhere.

# THREE

For Peter's second session, Dr. Terry rode his motorcycle to the Wyatt family's home in Bethlehem, Rhode Island, one hour south of Lexington. The seacoast town was being swallowed up by housing developments and fast-food franchises, but the Wyatts had money. They lived on a farm on a hill overlooking the original Yankee village that spawned the suburb. Coming up the long driveway, Terry rode through an open gate and past a horse grazing in a paddock.

The boy's father came out of the house and down the steps, and met Dr. Terry as he got off his Triumph.

"I'm Howard Wyatt, Dr. Canyon. Thank you so much for coming all this way to see Peter."

Dr. Terry took the father's hand. "No trouble at all, Judge Wyatt. This is a beautiful spot you have here."

"Pete's never been in trouble, you know. He's a sweetheart. Late baby, doted on by his mother and older sisters. He's been a little moody the last year or two, but I wrote that off to adolescence and Cathy and Sally being gone. He spends a lot of time in his room playing the guitar. Seems to have lost interest in sports."

Dr. Terry asked Judge Wyatt what he made of Peter's story of being spiked with LSD.

The judge measured the psychiatrist before he answered. "I think we know that was an improvisation. Peter had been acting strangely before the day of the incident."

Judge Wyatt was anxious to learn how he could help. Sensing his concern, the doctor said, "Most times stuff like this is just a phase. No long-term issues. Pete probably just got walloped by puberty. The hair starts springing out all over and the disposition goes to hell, right? Once he gets a girlfriend he'll find his balance again."

The father put his hand on the doctor's shoulder and drew close. "Monday of last week he came to breakfast speaking like a different person. He was . . . bemused. He asked me questions about my job, my life, what car I was driving. He stood over his mother and watched her cook. I thought he was going to weep. Then he gathered himself and sat down."

"Did he say he was from the future?"

"Not until the next day. He asked me to drive him to school, and he explained that he was an old man from the next century who had somehow been—he said 'rewound'—to his childhood and wanted me to know how much he loved seeing me again."

"And that day he took his clothes off in school?"

"The day after that."

The door to the house opened and Peter and his mother stepped out to greet their guest.

"Hey, Pete!" Dr. Terry said warmly.

"Hello, Doctor," the boy said. "Welcome to our 1970 house. No Wi-Fi, no cable, no Cialis. We live the primitive life of the frontier."

They all went inside. The father said quietly to the doctor, "These things he says—there's a kind of poetry to them."

"He's a very bright boy," Dr. Terry said. "That will be a big help. He's smart enough to navigate his way through."

With forced cheer the parents left Peter and his therapist in the library and closed the door. Dr. Terry could smell cookies baking.

He said, "How was the first day back?"

"Not as tough as I expected," Peter said. "A certain interest in the crazy kid. They all loved the acid story. Only the ones who've actually taken acid suspect it's bullshit. Here's the good thing—adolescents are supernaturally self-centered. Most of them have reverted to studying their reflections. My hallucinogen-fueled exhibitionism will certainly be what they think of when they think of me, but they won't spend an inordinate amount of time thinking about me. That's my guess."

"You got a way with words, dude," the doctor said.

Peter looked at him curiously. "I didn't think people said *dude* in 1970. I would have guessed that came in a few years later."

Dr. Terry took out one of his little cigars. "I'm ahead of the pack."

Peter looked vulnerable. "I'm watching for anachronisms. Anything to suggest this is all a fantasy. At first I figured I was dreaming. Two days in I decided I was in a coma. If something doesn't open up soon, I'm going to start believing I've died and what I'm experiencing is the last flicker of a decaying consciousness."

"That's a very negative way of looking at it."

"I mean, bear with me. I've considered the metaphysical option too. Wake up in your own childhood and everything is on the table. Am I in heaven? You'd think someone would tell you. Hell? Come on—smell those cookies."

"Purgatory?" the doctor asked.

"Is purgatory like *The Twilight Zone*? That's what I really feel. I keep expecting Rod Serling to step out from behind the fern."

The doctor wanted to steer the conversation from the abstract to the concrete. "What happened in school yesterday, Pete? What stands out?"

Peter looked like he was annoyed for a moment and then settled.

"Daphne Burrows," he said. "Girl in my class. My madness appeals to her. She slit her finger open to get my attention."

Concern crossed Dr. Terry's face. Pete said, "Nothing serious. Just a prick to make a point."

"Daphne a friend of yours?"

"Not at all. She's out of my league, and that's a good thing. Right now she's a precocious little troublemaker, but I remember what's ahead for her. Every year of high school Daphne got more beautiful, and every year she got wilder. She was very thin, and by junior year she was five ten. High cheekbones, full lips, a spray of freckles across her nose, and long, straight red hair that she parted in the center."

Dr. Terry said, "You're talking about her in the past tense."

"I have to distinguish the Daphne I saw yesterday from what I remember of her over the next few years."

"Future Daphne."

"Future to you, Doctor. Almost fifty years ago to me. As high school progressed Daphne experimented with opium, had an affair with a thirty-year-old music teacher, and dated a succession of rebels and troublemakers. Sophomore year she was with the radical leftist who wanted to form a high school chapter of Students for a Democratic Society. She dumped him for a knife-fighting juvenile delinquent. When we were seniors she was going steady with the school amphetamine addict. She broke each of their hearts in turn. In ninth grade she was just getting started."

The doctor asked what became of her after graduation.

"She might have grown up to be a brain surgeon," the boy said, "or she might have become an assassin. She vanished after high school, and no one I knew ever heard anything about her again. She's one of the great What-Ifs."

"Sounds like she made a big impression on you."

"Sucking her bloody finger at me got my attention, all right."

Peter rubbed his mouth with the back of his hand and looked at the therapist with concentration.

"She obviously made an impression on me when I was a kid. You think that's why I've given her a prominent role in this, uh, this delusion?"

Dr. Terry considered three or four conversational paths before choosing, "For the sake of clarity we have to consider the 'delusion' to be your memories of being a sixtysomething-year-old man from 2020."

"Sixty-five."

"Okay. I'm not making a value judgment here. I'm just trying to agree on a shared vocabulary. The delusion is the time travel stuff. You going to high school yesterday in 1970 and seeing this girl Daphne—we have to refer to that as reality."

"My shrink in 2020 isn't going to go for that," Peter said.

"Well, fuck him, dude, he's not even born yet."

Peter laughed. The doctor decided he was going to have

to pull over and write all this down as soon as he got out of the driveway.

"It's nice being here, Dr. Canyon," Peter said. "In a lot of ways it feels more real than my real life did. But I gotta get home."

"You sure you're not home already, Pete?"

"I miss my wife, Terry. I miss my children. If they don't exist, I'm going to crack up for real."

# FOUR

Moe Mosspaw got to school before dawn. He arrived at 5:15, ran the track for half an hour, showered in the boys' locker room, and took a coffee and newspaper into his office. It was a little after 6:00 a.m. He was surprised to find Mrs. Wyatt waiting for him. He figured she wanted to talk to him at a time when not many people would see her. How she had known he would be in his office so early, he had no idea.

"I appreciate your support during Peter's difficulties, Mr. Mosspaw," she told him.

"He seems to be getting back into the swing of things," the guidance counselor said. He felt embarrassed as soon as he said it. It sounded like boilerplate parent-teacher talk.

She said, "Children can be cruel. If Peter is picked on or mocked, I need you to let me know. His father and I are still unsure that his returning to this school is the right choice for him."

It occurred to Moe Mosspaw that it might make his own life easier if Peter Wyatt were to switch to another school, but he was bound to tell the mother the truth.

"I think he's doing okay, really. The kids understand someone slipped him something and he had a bad trip. It's scary, but it wasn't his fault."

Joanne Wyatt did not reply. She nodded. She seemed on the verge of saying something and then reconsidered. Finally, she asked what she could do to help Mr. Mosspaw help her son.

"He's seeing the psychiatrist? The fella from Harvard?"

"Dr. Canyon, yes. Twice a week."

Moe said, "Would it be okay if I sat down with Dr. Canyon at some point?"

Mrs. Wyatt was surprised. She asked what Mosspaw thought that would accomplish.

"Oh, you know . . . just to compare notes. The day shift talking to the night shift. I mean, if you don't think it's a good idea . . ."

"I think it's fine. Let's all get on the same wavelength. Shall I have Dr. Canyon reach out to you?"

"Or I could call him."

"I don't know if he will have any objection. Better if he calls you, I think."

"Sure."

A bell rang. The first bus was pulling up outside. Joanne Wyatt stood and thanked the guidance counselor for taking the time and for protecting Peter's interests.

She drove out of the parking lot before her son's school bus pulled in.

Peter had gym first period. In the showers afterward a loudmouth announced to the entire naked class, "Look out, everybody! Wyatt's got his wiener out again!"

The other students waited for his reaction. Peter laughed, disappointing them.

He was late to biology. He told the teacher he wasn't used to showering, toweling off, and getting dressed in the five minutes allotted. The teacher was a sleepy-eyed man named Houlihan whose gravy-stained necktie made it halfway down his enormous belly. He would not have accepted that excuse from most kids, but he understood that Wyatt was nuts.

Houlihan stood before a large pull-down rendering of the periodic table from the chemistry class he taught the period before. He read aloud from the textbook in a monotone. The boy looked at the clock and tried to comprehend that he was an hour and twenty minutes into a six-hour school day. It was like swimming through pancake batter.

There was a knock at the classroom door. A tall girl with short, curly hair entered. She carried a spiral notebook and a knapsack pimpled with little smile buttons.

"Mr. Houlihan," she said, "I'm Delores Marx from the student council. I'm here to make the announcement?"

The science teacher was not a man who read the daily notices in the teachers' lounge except when they pertained to a meatloaf supper.

"The Ecology Club," Delores told him in a stage whisper.

Houlihan grunted and gave her the floor. Delores addressed the class while referring to a handful of lined note cards.

"A lot of you have heard the word *ecology* lately. You may ask what it means. Ecology is the system of life itself. It is the study of the intricate web of nature, from plants and animals to the animal known as man. Us. President Nixon has called on high school and college students to protect the precious environment and become active in cleaning up pollution and keeping our school, our town, and our nation beautiful."

A sleepy voice from the back of the room murmured, "And to make us forget about the war."

Delores pressed on: "Answering the president's challenge, West Beth Vets is starting its own ecology club. The first meeting will be tomorrow, right after school in the caf."

The sleepy voice came again: "Yeah, let's pick up our trash and burn it in a big incinerator. That'll help the environment."

Houlihan roused himself, climbed to his feet, and glared at the heckler.

"You got something to say to the class, DeVille? That's a first."

Ricky DeVille was slouched so far down in his chair he was almost underneath the lab table. Greasy hair fell across his tinted aviator glasses. He wore a long black leather coat over a black shirt, black jeans, and pointed black Mondo boots.

"Earth Day is a scam," DeVille said. He was looking at his desk but had raised his mumble loud enough that everyone could hear him. "The government wants kids to stop protesting the war so they figure they can divert our energy to picking up litter. It's all bullshit."

Mr. Houlihan came alive. He slammed his meaty fist on his desk and shouted, "You don't use profanity in my class, DeVille! Go to Vice Principal Lockwood's office right now!"

Ricky DeVille shrugged, gathered his books, and shambled out of the room.

Houlihan told Delores to go ahead.

She recited, "Please consider coming to the cafeteria immediately after school tomorrow to hear about the exciting plans of the West Beth Vets Ecology Club." She smiled, nodded, and left. She had many more classrooms to hit before the bell.

Houlihan went back to reading from the textbook. He was talking about ablation.

At his next session with Dr. Canyon, Peter was anxious to recount DeVille's rebellion.

"Ricky DeVille spoke in class," Peter said. "My hallucination has departed from reality. I expect to see leprechauns emerging from Pepsi cans and orangutans aloft on silver wings. It's all wide open now."

Dr. Terry asked Peter to tell him about Ricky DeVille.

"I was in school with Ricky for six years, and I never heard him speak to a teacher. He was the last of three DeVille brothers. The older two had caused plenty of trouble, and by the time Ricky came along there was a mutual nonaggression pact between the family and the faculty. The teachers would never call on Ricky, and he wouldn't cause any trouble."

"He was a pal of yours?"

"No. Only time I remember talking with him was when he found out I played guitar. We spent a gym class discussing Johnny Winter behind the bleachers when we were supposed to be running track. He smoked Winstons. Funny, the things you remember."

Dr. Terry asked what else Peter recalled about the DeVilles.

"Ricky's older brothers were health class legends! Man, I had forgotten about Health until I landed here. Four semesters of Scared Straight tales of teenagers who ruined their lives with unplanned pregnancies, shotgun marriages, and venereal diseases. Occasionally a local policeman would visit to give eyewitness accounts of early death and imprisonment brought on by glue sniffing, pot smoking, and pill popping among the adolescents of Bethlehem. We were regularly warned that even one toke of a marijuana cigarette could send us flying off the roof like Art Linkletter's daughter."

Dr. Terry considered that he should not have told his patient that he knew Timothy Leary.

Peter went on: "The policeman always reminded us that the town had set up a telephone number where you could anonymously give the cops information on drug dealers for a hundred-dollar reward. It was called the TIP Line—TIP stood for Turn In a Pusher. Here's where the DeVilles come in. Before the cops set up the TIP Line, a group of concerned students, parents, and guidance counselors had organized a different anonymous phone line to talk down kids who were having bad trips, were victims of abuse, or had other problems they couldn't bring to their parents or teachers. This service was called People in Trouble, or PIT. Delores Marx came up with the slogan 'Bad trip? Make a PIT Stop!'"

Peter looked at the therapist and said, "You see where this is going?"

Dr. Terry said, "No idea."

"The potential for confusion between the TIP Line and the PIT Line was obvious. Which is how Barry DeVille, Ricky's brother, ended up in Socko."

Dr. Terry's eyebrows rose.

"Sockanosset," Peter explained. "The state reformatory. One night before I got to high school, Barry DeVille ingested a bad shish kebab of PCP, STP, and horse tranquilizer. He crawled to the phone and asked the operator to connect him to the TIP

Line for help. He meant to ask for the PIT Line. Or maybe, as Barry always contended, the operator misunderstood him. He wasn't at his most articulate. Barry was put through to a Bethlehem narcotics officer who took down all his information, including what he had taken, where he got it, how much more he had access to, where that was deposited, and at which address they could come and collect him. This was deemed in court to be a voluntary confession and admissible evidence."

Peter was on his feet. Terry Canyon was wishing he used a tape recorder in therapy sessions. There was no way he was going to remember all this.

Peter said, "Barry DeVille cemented his status as a teenage legend at West Bethlehem when, after being sentenced to six months at the reformatory, the judge asked if he wanted to say anything to the court. Barry answered, 'Yeah—I turned in a druggie. Where's my hundred dollars?'"

Dr. Terry ran his hands through his thick hair and said, "That's a funny story, Pete. So that I have it straight—this all happened in this reality we're living in here, or this happened in your delusion?"

The smile left Peter's face. He said, "It never occurred to me that my memories from before 1970 wouldn't apply to this . . . uh . . . this version. I'm just getting used to the idea that the last fifty years of my life have been erased. I hope I can at least count on the first fifteen."

Dr. Terry's job was to row the boy back to shore, not push him farther out. He said, "I can look up Barry DeVille's record. See if it's the way you remember it. I'm a doctor—I can get away with all kinds of shit."

"Right." Peter looked sadder than the psychiatrist had seen him look before. He looked like he was drowning.

"I think I might have had a stroke," he said. "That would explain why this dream is enduring. Maybe I am in a coma, my wife begging the doctors to bring me out of it, my children imploring me to hang in, come back.

"My boy James would stay with me the whole time. I'm sure of that. He would be whispering in my ear, telling me they're with me. Jenny would take care of her mom. She'd be pummeling the doctors and nurses with questions. She's probably on Wikipedia, diagnosing my condition and coming up with experimental cures. Janice would be stoic. She wouldn't want the kids to see how worried she was. She'd give them jobs to keep them occupied. I'm afraid Janice and Jenny would create a vortex of escalating assignments for each other and the boys. That might cause Pete Junior to withdraw. He wouldn't know how to deal with my being comatose, and the chatter between his mom and his sister would send him out of the hospital and into his car to drive around until his head cleared. I just hope he doesn't start drinking."

Dr. Terry studied the boy. Peter lifted his fingers and wiggled them in front of his eyes. He slapped himself hard. Dr. Terry jumped but Peter held up his open hand to say it was okay. He said, "A stroke would explain it. My consciousness might be fleeing from blocked neural pathways down alternative synaptic corridors. I could be burning up these obscure storage centers looking for a trail back to clarity."

Dr. Terry said, "The way you talk, I almost find it plausible that you're a sixty-five-year-old man. What's hard for me to believe is that I'm a figment of your imagination. I mean, I'm conscious in here too."

"You'd have to say that, though, wouldn't you?" Peter said. "Look, Dr. Canyon, if any of these ninth-grade memories are useful as fuel to get me back to 2020, burn them up! Take them all! I never need to remember anything about 1970 again."

When their time was up, Terry Canyon said so long and put his hand on Peter's shoulder. Beneath his show-off vocabulary, the kid was really scared.

He walked out of the Wyatt house toward his Triumph. The days had gotten longer and the weather was warm. The air was sweet with blooming lilacs. Judge Wyatt came out of the house and approached him. Dr. Terry saw Mrs. Wyatt watching from the kitchen door.

"He's a brilliant kid, Mr. Wyatt," he told the father. "He could ace the verbal portion of the SATs tomorrow, that's for sure. He's able to articulate everything he's going through. I can't tell you how helpful that is."

The judge gave a tight smile and nodded, struggling to get out what he wanted to ask. "Is there a chance this might be physical?"

"What do you mean?"

The judge turned away from his wife and lowered his voice.

"There's no reason to check for a brain tumor, is there?" He looked ashamed of himself for saying the words.

"I really don't think so. I mean, I can order some tests if you want, but there's nothing to suggest anything like that. At all."

The judge nodded. "Good. Sure. Good. Just thinking of every possible—"

"I don't know what's going on in Peter's head exactly, sir," the doctor said. "But that kid's special. Once this is settled he's going to have a fantastic life."

The father said, "He's convinced he already has."

# FIVE

Dr. Terry took his Triumph down the long driveway and onto the street that ran to the interstate toward Massachusetts. He rode north four miles and took the exit. He had another appointment in Rhode Island. The boy's mother had asked him to meet with the school guidance counselor.

Moe Mosspaw suggested they rendezvous at a Howard Johnson's off the highway. The restaurant was easy to find. Dr. Terry pulled up next to a brown Subaru. The driver was sitting behind the wheel. He looked at Terry and said, "Taking a trip?"

"Come again?"

The driver was a man in his late thirties with a pointed nose, high forehead, and horn-rimmed glasses. "Taking a trip? You know—*Then Came Bronson*. 'Taking a trip? Wherever I end up, I guess.' You're Dr. Canyon?"

"Guilty."

"I'm Moe Mosspaw."

"Nice to meet you, Moe."

"Thank you for making time, Doctor."

"Call me Terry. Let's get some clams."

They found a booth in the back of the restaurant and got coffee. Dr. Terry ordered a clam roll. Moe Mosspaw asked for a BLT. They talked about Peter Wyatt without using his name, in case anyone was listening.

"Have you followed the research in frontal lobe development in adolescents, Doctor?" Mosspaw asked when the food arrived.

"I might have missed class that day."

"It's fascinating stuff," the guidance counselor said. "Well, it's fascinating if you spend fifty hours a week dealing with the problems of teenagers. There are arguments about exactly how this works, but in a nutshell, you know, the frontal lobe is the brain's policeman. Reason, self-control, patience. That's all frontal lobe stuff."

"You mind if I smoke, Moe?"

"Not a bit. The bottom of the brain, that's primal stuff. Impulses. Me hungry, me horny, me angry, me sleepy. During adolescence both parts of the brain are growing at a rapid rate. The whole time the brain is expanding, it's also laying pipe between the different regions to carry messages."

"Links."

"Exactly. The axons are the lines that carry signals from one part of the brain to the other. Myelin greases some of the axons. But here's the snafu—the entire brain doesn't grow at the same rate. From about thirteen till eighteen the back section, the lizard brain, is firing like the Fourth of July, demanding sensation, lighting up the libido, begging to break the speed limit. The frontal lobe, home of restraint and reason, is the last place to get fully wired. We get mad with these kids for acting out, for making dumb, impulsive decisions. But that's how their brains are designed. It's only when they grow up that the lights go on in the front room and order is restored."

Dr. Terry tipped back his head and dropped a fried clam in his mouth, saying as he chewed, "In my game we call this the id, the ego, and the superego. Curly, Larry, and Moe. Curly the id wants to go wild. Larry the ego is embarrassed. Moe the superego slaps Curly and pokes him in the eye. You're saying that for the average teenager, Moe has no mojo."

"Right—Curly is running the show."

Dr. Terry tried to work out what this had to do with Peter Wyatt. He said, "You deal with a great many kids, the majority of whom are statistically normal. I deal with a small sample who are brought to see me because they have issues."

"In my experience," Mosspaw said, "all adolescents have issues."

Dr. Terry agreed that was probably true. To get to see him, a kid had to have not only flipped out severely—he also had to have parents who could and would engage a psychiatrist. Mr. Mosspaw dealt with fifty times the adolescents Dr. Terry did.

"Whatever is causing our boy's situation," Terry said, "it's not a lack of higher brain function. He talks so rationally, lucidly, he almost makes me wonder . . ." Dr. Terry paused. He wasn't free to discuss Peter's delusion with the guidance counselor.

Mosspaw asked him, "What were you going to say?"

"I know that a kid taking off his clothes in math class suggests a suspension of normal inhibitions. But in this subject's case I think the appropriate axons are fully greased and logic is in the pilot's seat. What I'm working on is if that logic is proceeding from a flawed premise."

Moe Mosspaw had nothing but good intentions. His request to meet with the boy's psychiatrist came from a sincere effort to understand what was going on with Peter and find the best solution for him while protecting all the students of West Bethlehem Veterans Memorial High School. It was the sort of above-and-beyond obligation Mosspaw assumed all the time. He did his best to put aside any worry that he was out of his depth talking adolescent psychology with a Harvard psychiatrist. Terry Canyon had treated him as an equal from the moment they sat down, but Mosspaw had lost the thread.

"What is the flawed premise you think Peter—sorry, the subject—is operating under?"

Dr. Terry flashed a smile and said, "That's what I'm working on figuring out. Hey, you gonna eat those fries?"

The gate between them came down.

# SIX

Peter found fifteen dollars in his dresser and walked into town to the record store. He came back up the driveway with three new LPs: Miles Davis's *Bitches Brew*, Emitt Rhodes's self-titled first album, and *John, the Wolf King of L.A.* He opened the kitchen door and saw his mother standing, stirring cake mix in a bowl and smiling at him with an expression between delight and conspiracy. He followed her gaze to the kitchen table, where Daphne Burrows sat drinking a cup of coffee, a bandage on her slit finger.

"Your friend came by to see you, Peter," his mother said.

"I wanted to see if you had the homework from math," Daphne told him like no one was even supposed to believe it.

Peter was pretty sure this was the first time a girl from school had appeared at his home since his classmates got too old to trick or treat. His mother was beaming. Daphne was wearing a tan shirt with pearl buttons and loose silver bracelets on both wrists. She was lovely. Peter was sad to see how hopeful this surprise visit made his mom. She had to be thinking, "Maybe my boy is normaling up." She didn't know that Daphne was an engine of destruction. Sipping her coffee, she looked like the sweetest girl in the world.

"You live in such a nice place, Peter," Daphne said. "I had no idea there was all this land up here." She turned to his mother and explained, "We live over in Buttongreen. Rows of ranch houses."

"Buttongreen is beautiful," Peter's mother said, working the cake batter like a throttle. "These old houses, something's always breaking. I often wish we lived in a new home."

Daphne said, "Would you show me around, Peter?"

Peter would have said yes to anything to get her away from his mother. He put down his records and held open the screen door. She picked up a large cloth handbag with Apache braiding, thanked Mrs. Wyatt for the coffee, and followed him out the door.

They walked across the driveway and through a gate in the stone wall toward the horse barn.

"Your mother seems sane," Daphne said. "Do you get your craziness from your father?"

Peter said, "I'm sui generis. What brings you here, Daphne?"

"Homework."

"Five or six kids from algebra class live in your neighborhood."

"Don't you like me coming by?"

"I'm very flattered."

"Something smells like perfume."

"Hyacinths. My mother plants them. They're blooming now."

She reached into her Indian handbag and brought out a small bottle of vodka. She unscrewed the top, took a swig, and held it out for Peter.

He said, "Daphne, you're fifteen years old."

She said, "Not for three and a half months."

"Stop it."

"Have you ever had a drink, Peter?"

"Daphne, I've had every inebriant from tequila in Guadalajara to absinthe in Morocco."

"You really are crazy." She took another swallow and wiped her mouth on the hand with the bandaged finger. They arrived at the horse barn and the boy unhitched and swung open the upper door of the first stall. A smoke-colored horse with a charcoal mane pushed his large head out and nuzzled him. The boy became emotional.

"Rooke," he said to the horse. "How are you, fella? It's good to see you again. It's good to see you." He ran his hand behind the horse's ear and said, "We should get him some oats."

Daphne asked him, "Why are you upset?"

"I haven't seen Rooke in a long time."

"Don't you live here?"

Peter led her to the tack shop at the end of the barn. There were saddles mounted on short beams coming out of the wall and a black potbellied stove in the center of the room. He opened a grain drawer and scooped out some oats into a coffee can. They went back outside, and he showed her how to hold her hand flat and let the horse take them. At the first lick of the animal's big tongue she squealed and dropped the oats on the ground. Peter scooped them up and fed them to the horse.

"He won't bite you, you don't have to worry," he told her. "He just can't see very well."

"Is that all he eats?" she asked.

"He eats hay."

"Can we feed him hay?"

"He's already eaten."

"Please? A little?"

Peter shrugged and led her up a flight of wooden stairs to the hayloft. It was stuffy. It felt like a hundred degrees. The boy told her to watch her head on the beams and follow him. She grabbed his hand and stuck close. They entered a room stacked with hay bales, and he hauled open a wooden door on rollers to let in fresh air and light. He bent to grab a bale of hay. She took a long drink of vodka and said, "Do you ever make out up here?"

He didn't turn to look at her. He said, "You'd come away with a rash. This hay is like a thousand needles."

"Needles in a haystack," she said. She put her hand on the back of his neck. He looked at her. She had unbuttoned her shirt. She had a black ballet top underneath. Peter got flustered.

She said, "I'm hot."

"Let's feed the horse."

"Aren't you hot? Take off your shirt, Peter."

"Stop it, Daphne."

"Have a drink."

He stood up straight. She pushed against him, belly to belly. Peter was red-faced. Daphne Burrows was excited. When she kissed him, he was vibrating. Lust boiled in him like lava getting ready to blow. He felt every part of his body becoming erect, his spine stiffening and his brain swelling in his skull. Blood filled his eyes. Just when he was certain that nothing could stop this explosion, a thought came screaming across his mind: If he gave in to Daphne now, he would cut all ties to his wife and children. He would be gone into 1970 forever. He would never get home.

As Daphne reached for his belt he grabbed her wrist hard and whispered, "This can't happen."

She said, "It's happening already."

"No," Peter insisted. He squeezed her wrist and pushed her away from him. "You're fourteen years old. Fourteen! Do you understand what that means?"

"I'm fifteen in August."

"Listen to me, Daphne. You're a child! If you don't change your behavior, you'll head toward a lot of trouble!"

He sounded like her grandmother, she thought, but he looked like he wanted to throw her on the hay pile.

She said, "You don't have to be scared, Peter."

"I'm terrified! I don't want to be here, and I don't want you to be here."

She said, "A little vodka would help you feel better."

He struggled to say anything, and when he did it was, "Listen to me, Daphne. I'm married!"

It hit Daphne that perhaps she should be a little scared herself. She understood the boy was crazy. She hadn't understood what crazy really was. Peter rolled the wooden door shut, walked out of the room, and waited for her on the steps. She took a minute to button her shirt, brush off her clothes, and put the top back on the vodka. She hoisted the Apache handbag onto her shoulder and followed him out of the barn.

When Peter came back into the kitchen his mother asked if his friend was staying for dinner. He said she left.

"She seemed very nice. Have you known her long?"

"I guess I have, yeah. A long time."

"Did you help her with her homework?"

"Not really."

"Well, she seemed very nice."

"Yeah."

"It's good for you to have friends your own age to talk to, Peter."

He looked at his mother with something close to grief. He said, "No one is my age, Mom."

# SEVEN

The boy's mother called Dr. Canyon and asked for an emergency session. Peter was the worst he had been. The doctor said he had other patients, but if they wanted to come to Massachusetts he would fit the boy in at the end of the day. At 6 p.m. Peter was at his door.

"I don't believe I can hold it together anymore," Peter told him. "Daphne tried to get me to have sex with her."

Dr. Terry asked if they did anything. Peter said, "She's a little girl for God's sake."

"She's your age, Pete."

The boy glared at him and said, "Respect my delusion. I'm sixty-five years old in here! In 2020 I get aroused about once every full moon. But now, this body—fuck, it's like I'm in a hormone swamp. I didn't remember how horny fifteen-year-olds are. My sex life has been on a gentle decline for twenty-five years, and now it all comes rushing back at once and I can't do anything. It's maddening!"

This was a delicate call. Dr. Terry said, "I'm not condoning underage sex, Pete, but—you know, a little petting is normal."

Peter exploded. "You're going to counsel a disturbed adolescent to have sex with a fourteen-year-old? You should lose your license, you charlatan!"

Dr. Terry was surprised by Peter's anger. His delusion could be progressing toward psychosis. Time to take a chance. He said, "Tell me about your wife, Peter."

"Fuck off back to Zabriskie Point, you hippie! We have something where I come from called the MeToo movement, Terry. Old men who try to have sex with young girls don't fare well in 2020."

The doctor said, "I need to understand the world you believe you come from."

"We pay for water and television."

"Tell me about your wife."

"Janice."

"Tell me about Janice."

"I don't trust you, Terry."

"You don't have to. Where do you and Janice live?"

"In Tribeca."

"Where is Tribeca?"

"It's a neighborhood in lower Manhattan. We have a house in Westchester. Since the kids left, we spend more time in the city."

"How many children do you have?"

"Three."

"What do you do for a living?"

The boy was mistrustful. Dr. Terry picked up a pen and a leather notebook. He flipped it open and gestured for Peter to talk.

"I spent most of my career in radio."

"Deejay?"

"Programmer. Now I work for a streaming service."

"What's that?"

"Doesn't matter."

"When did you meet Janice?"

"I was thirty. She was twenty-five. She was playing in a band. The Bouviers. They weren't much, but she was fantastic. A police chief's daughter from Long Island. Smartest person I ever met."

"You loved music so much you married a musician."

"We fall in love with people who are what we wish to be."

Dr. Terry made a note of that. It calmed Peter to talk about the world he thought he had left. After ten minutes of circling, he spoke freely about the life he believed he had lost.

"For a long while time passed slowly," Peter said. "High school, college, moving to New York. It was like every month lasted a year. Until Janice and I got married. Then we went into life's carpool lane. We had twins, a boy and a girl. Janice quit her band. I got a promotion. A friend of mine told me, 'Children bring money. They leave you no choice.' We took the kids to preschool. We went on family trips. I worked hard and attended lots of meetings. It was always almost Christmas or almost summer vacation. We had another boy and named him Peter after me. We moved to the house in Westchester but kept the apartment downtown. Our kids became teenagers and gave us the usual grief. I changed jobs for more money. We got a cat, and then we got a dog, too. We went to PTA meetings, school plays, tennis lessons, swim meets, and basketball games. Our parents got old, and we helped take care of them until they died."

The boy was choking up. Dr. Terry stopped writing. He closed his notebook and said, "Just talk."

"One minute we're watching *The Little Mermaid*, and the next we're going on university tours. Jenny went to college in

North Carolina. James stayed close—NYU. People warned us about the empty nest, but Peter was at home, usually with a houseful of cronies, and James was nearby, and Jenny was back half the year, and the dog was barking at the cat, and I was busy. The nest felt full to me.

"Until the day we left the youngest at college in California. On the flight back to New York Janice and I looked at each other, and it hit us. That's it. The baby is out of the house. That chapter is over. And the strange thing about it was that the chapter I've just described didn't feel like it took any longer than high school or college had. The three decades we spent as parents with kids in the house felt like four years, more or less. But when I looked up I was sixty and my hair was turning white. Janice is younger than I am, but in photographs we looked like old people. She called us the Van Winkles.

"I started having dreams in which the past and future were mixed up. I'd be with my kids as they are in their twenties but with my parents still young. Or I'd be back in school but my wife would be there too. I enjoyed those dreams. It was like I was taping over old memories and they were bleeding through. That's why, when I woke up in my childhood bedroom in 1970, I played along. I thought it was another of those dreams. The most vivid yet. It took me a long time to realize I couldn't get out."

Peter stopped talking. He sat back and stared at a Navajo mask on the wall.

Terry Canyon spoke quietly. "I want you to go somewhere with me, Peter. Consider this. When you were in 2020, you had your wife and children, but your parents were gone, right? They were a memory."

"Yes."

"Even though your parents, whom you loved, were dead, you were generally happy?"

"Yes. I was happy. I had my children and Janice."

"I know how much you want them back. I can't see inside your delusion, Peter, but I know it's as real to you as this table. They're as real to you as I am."

"They're more real to me than you are."

"In 2020 you had your wife and kids but your parents were a memory. And that memory gave you comfort. Now you're in 1970. Janice and the children are not here physically but they are alive in your memory. And your parents are with you again. You're not alone."

Peter put his head in his hands. "It's not a fair trade."

Dr. Terry said, "I know it's not, Pete. But it might be a way to think about it that doesn't hurt so much. It might be a way to hang on."

Peter held his fists against his eyes. Dr. Terry put a hand on his shoulder, and they sat that way without speaking for a long time. Finally, Peter looked up at the clock. It was ten past seven. His mother would be outside. He looked at Dr. Terry evenly and asked if this session replaced Saturday.

The doctor said no, Saturday was still on. This was a bonus.

"Okay," Peter said, brushing his hair back. "See you Saturday."

"Count on it."

At the door Peter stopped and said, "If I remain stuck here, I'll have to do everything exactly the same to get back to my old life. I'll have to duplicate every step."

Dr. Terry said, "That makes sense, I guess."

"But see, I've already changed it. I didn't become the school lunatic the first time. I didn't strip naked in front of the class; I didn't go to a psychiatrist. I never heard of Dr. Terry Canyon. Daphne Burrows never came over to my house and tried to seduce me in the hayloft. I've already ruined it."

"You haven't ruined anything, Pete. You might be able to make it come out better."

"No," the boy said evenly. "I've ruined it. I had it perfect the first time, but I had to lose it to know."

# EIGHT

The window of the school bus was fallout-shelter-sign yellow, stained with seasons of spit, snot, and sweat. Peter leaned his head against the glass and studied the town passing by. At the end of World War II, Bethlehem had been a collection of small farms circling a half dozen mill villages. Each village had a main street with a grocer, a cobbler, a barber, a hardware store, a bank, an auto-repair shop, and a beauty parlor. Each village had at least one church, one bar, and one place to eat. Each village had a grammar school. Half the villages had small department stores that sold clothes, shoes, and home furnishings. Two had movie theaters. Two had libraries. One had a tailor. One had a print shop. Doctors and dentists had offices in each village. The two high schools, West Beth and East Beth, were built between the villages on what had been farmland.

The farms became suburbs in the fifties. Young families filled up the new housing developments. In 1970 Peter could see the old Bethlehem under the new plats and widened streets and gas stations. He could also see what was coming: roads expanding to highways to carry commuters from all over the state to the new malls, the office parks, the multiplex theaters. The next few years would bring apartment buildings along the shore for bachelors, spinsters, and widows, followed by cheap multifamily units behind the train tracks. Along the way would come strip malls and 7-Elevens, every evolution of McDonald's, Burger King, IHOP, Friendly's, Wendy's, TGI Fridays, Taco Bell, Ruby Tuesdays. Video stores would come and go. Then big box stores as the malls got old and began to fail. With the introduction of internet commerce many of the big box stores would be abandoned. The apartment buildings would fall into disrepair. Weeds would grow through cracks in the concrete. By the 1990s immigrants from Cape Verde, Southeast Asia, and Central America would move in and do their best to make lives for their families, while Peter's generation's daughters and sons would move back to the cities their grandparents fled. Peter could see the map of what used to be bleeding through the map of what was coming as the school bus rolled onto the grounds of West Bethlehem Veterans Memorial High.

He saw something else. A group of about a dozen students were waiting to greet the buses. They were all wearing black armbands. Among them was Daphne Burrows.

"US out of Cambodia!" a boy with frizzy Dylan hair shouted as the bus doors opened to let the students out.

"Stop shooting kids!" a girl yelled.

Daphne spotted Peter and pushed forward to hand him an armband. She looked him in the eye and said, "No more Kent States!"

Peter felt as if he had been in a silent room and someone turned up the volume. The chants of the teenagers knocked him back. He said to Daphne, "Kent State—when did it happen?"

"You really are loco, aren't you, Peter? When did it happen? It happened yesterday. Did you pass out in the hayloft? It's the only thing on the news. Students are going on strike across the country. All the colleges are closing." She was lit up like Christmas. "High schools are going to be next!"

Peter accepted the black armband and moved toward the school as Vice Principal Lockwood, Mosspaw, and a pair of gym teachers rushed to break up the radicals before they could rally any more buses. Peter headed to the pay phone by the nurse's office and dialed Terry Canyon collect.

The psychiatrist was in a net hammock on his front porch in Lexington, shoeless, writing in his leather notebook with a calligrapher's pen. His secretary told him that Peter Wyatt was calling, distraught. Terry went inside and took the phone.

"What's happening, Pete?"

"Doctor. Kent State—those four kids. I could have warned someone! I wasn't even thinking . . . Jesus, my self-absorption . . . I was so obsessed with my own selfish . . . I could have done something."

The psychiatrist's voice was even: "You didn't mention anything about this to me, Pete."

"That's what I'm saying! It was so long ago it didn't occur to me I could change it. But I could have. Maybe that's why I was put here—to save those kids. I was put here and I didn't do anything to help!"

"Pete. Buddy. Listen. What could you have done? Who could you have told? Who'd have believed you?"

"I could have called the college, the dorms."

"Peter, if some crazy—forgive me, buddy—if some crazy kid had started calling the dorms on that campus saying the National Guard were going to shoot the demonstrators, the only possible consequence I can see is that you would have made things worse."

Peter asked, "What could be worse?"

"Four students got killed for holding up signs. Imagine if they'd armed themselves. Could have been more people shot."

Peter sat down on the linoleum floor holding the receiver. Dr. Terry kept talking: "You couldn't have changed anything."

"You don't know that."

"Where are you?"

"School."

"Tell you what. For our next session you write down for me every tragedy, every disaster, every bad thing that's coming in the next six months, and we'll discuss whether any of them can be prevented and how we can try to do that."

"Okay."

"Okay?"

"Yes, Doctor. Thank you."

The bell rang. A gym teacher rushed by, dragging Ricky DeVille by the black armband. Peter hung up the phone.

In Lexington, Dr. Terry went back to his hammock and picked up his notebook. He flipped to the page with his musings about the strange case of Peter Wyatt. He began to scribble. Today he was considering right brain/left brain disjunction. Most people's hemispheres were in sync most of the time, but there was a theory that a slight stutter between left and right sides could be responsible for déjà vu, the illusion that one had experienced an event before. The theory was that the event was registering in one hemisphere a split second before the other. In extreme cases the subject began hearing voices. Déjà vu became schizophrenia. Dr. Terry was open to all possibilities, but the great probability was that the boy didn't warn anyone about the Kent State shootings because he didn't know they were going to happen until he heard the news, at which point he was overwhelmed with the belief he had known it already. If this were true, something in the boy's wiring was circling on itself. He was mistaking an echo for an experience.

In math class Peter stared at his notebook and considered the assignment Dr. Terry had given him. He made circles on the page with his pen and tried to remember what came next. They were heading into the summer of 1970. What happened in the summer of 1970? The assassinations were over. Man had walked on the moon. Teddy Kennedy had driven off the bridge. The Mets had won the '69 World Series. Woodstock and Altamont and Manson had entered the public vocabulary. A lot of history happened in 1969. But May of 1970? The Beatles broke up the month before. Apollo 13 made it back to Earth. What big news event was impending that Peter could use to prove he was from 2020?

He could think of nothing. Did that mean that nothing memorable happened in the world in the summer after Kent State, or did it mean he was truly deluded? Were his memories between age fifteen and sixty-five a dream so vivid that it was trying to take over his life? If he could accept that—if he could simply act as if he accepted it—he might haul himself out of this chasm.

What other option did he have?

Daphne Burrows arrived in class late and raging. Ordered to remove the black band from her arm, she had wrapped it around her head. She took the seat next to Peter and whispered, "The pigs won't win this one."

The math teacher said, "You're late, Miss Burrows."

"Mr. Wood," she said evenly, "I was denied my right to protest an unjust war."

"Don't set yourself on fire in the quadrangle and I won't give you detention," the teacher said, and wrote an equation on the chalkboard. He was coming around the greater-than sign when the public address system crackled awake with the voice of Delores Marx, the earnest girl from the Ecology Club with the smile buttons on her knapsack.

"Attention all students and faculty. There has been much concern expressed about the sad events at Kent State University and what it might mean for our own schedule and graduation exercises. We all feel for the families of the students who were slain and injured in this terrible tragedy, and for the National Guardsmen who are now being subjected to so much criticism. Vice Principal Lockwood wants to stress that while we all are upset, any talk of student strikes or walkouts will be treated as truancy. There will be a special meeting during E period today to give us a chance to talk through our feelings, share songs and poetry inspired by our emotional pain, and quell any anxieties we share."

Peter was struck by Delores's use of *quell*. This was a statement drafted by a committee for sure. Delores was the sort of level-headed student the faculty would choose to deal with in a touchy situation, rather than risk the little Che Guevaras expressing their dissent with obscenities and eggs. It would be unkind to call Delores the class quisling, the boy considered, but not entirely unfair.

The announcement went on: "We would like to ask each class to elect two student reps to come to the small auditorium today at two for an open discussion about this event, which is of concern to us all. Teachers, please ask your classes to vote for their student representatives at this time and send their names to Mr. Mosspaw, who will chair the discussion. Thank you."

Well, that's going to do those dead kids a lot of good, Peter thought, and went back to trying to remember something significant that happened in the summer of 1970 that he could use to prove he was not insane. The class began chattering about who should represent them at the Kent State meeting. Daphne put up her hand to volunteer, and in a smooth gesture slipped the black armband out of her hair and onto her raised arm. She was picked by the other kids, none of whom gave any sign of wishing to share the honor.

Peter did not at first register Daphne's saying, "I nominate Peter Wyatt to be the other class rep."

Peter heard a general moan from his classmates. He was, after all, the school wacko.

He said, "I don't really . . ."

Daphne said, "Vote for Wyatt! If the administration tries to shut us up, he'll take his clothes off on the evening news!" The students laughed, and hands shot up to make Peter their second delegate.

The math teacher looked pained. He said, "You want to be our rep, Peter?"

Peter was a thousand miles from shore. What could he do but ride the wave?

"Sure, Mr. Wood. I'll go."

He sensed the same muted disappointment from his classmates he had felt when he returned to class after the scandal and failed to act like a maniac. If they had to go to school with a crazy kid, did he have to be so boring?

Daphne was delighted. When the teacher picked up the black phone on the wall to give the office the names of his two student reps, she reached over and punched the boy on the shoulder. "Bastille Day," she whispered.

It gave Peter a flash of apprehension. What if 1970 were only the first stop on a backward journey? He could wake up tomorrow in the Reign of Terror, riding a tumbrel to the guillotine. And Daphne—he could picture Daphne sitting in the front row knitting while blood sprayed her dress and his head flopped into her basket.

# NINE

The rest of the morning passed in systemic lethargy. When the bell rang at two, Peter peeled off from the mob zombie-marching down the corridor and moved toward the Kent State meeting in the small auditorium at the center of campus.

West Bethlehem Veterans Memorial High School was laid out like a hobbled swastika. The principal's office, school staff rooms, and the two auditoriums were in the middle of the structure. Four long corridors designated wings A, B, C, and D shot out from that hub. Two of those wings bent left at their ends, creating E and F wings. Three cinderblock classrooms in a windowless pillbox outside the fire doors of F wing formed the outpost of G wing. Health classes were held out there—sex education being segregated by design or accident from the body of the school.

Peter made it to the small auditorium and leaned against the back wall. Daphne arrived at the center of a cluster of alpha girls. She was telling them, "It's not like they're ever going to let us do anything that would actually address what's really going on in this fucked-up country, right?"

Daphne's friend Pasa said, "Do you realize the Boston Massacre was exactly two hundred years ago? British troops opened fire on a group of protestors and killed five of them. It started the Revolutionary War."

Pasa wore granny glasses and high-waisted corduroy slacks. Peter couldn't remember her real name but recalled that she'd adopted Pasa as a protest. It stood for People Against Spiro Agnew. The school jocks thought it was funny to call out "*¿Qué Pasa?*" when she went by. To them she said it stood for "People Against Stupid Assholes."

Daphne's group took seats at single-arm desks and watched the room fill up. As freshmen they were at the bottom of the social slope. Condescending seniors, self-serious juniors, and smirking sophomores rolled in and commanded the good positions. It was unusual for representatives of all four classes to be in one gathering. Some of the ninth graders were only fourteen, while the older twelfth graders were already eighteen, the longest four-year gap in the human life span.

Peter wondered what threats of walkouts or disruption had inspired the administration to convene this meeting. Was it a directive from the mayor's office? Was the superintendent of schools panicked that the televised riots on college campuses in the wake of the events at Kent State would inspire an enraged archery team to volley flaming arrows at the faculty lounge? West Beth High had only recently relaxed the dress code to allow girls to wear pants to school and boys to have hair below their ears. It was no incubator of radicalism.

A scrum of sullen seniors in defiant black armbands marched in together and reconnoitered the room. From out of the middle of their group emerged a fierce young woman with frizzy black hair and a hawk nose. Peter knew her at once: Mina Habib, strident voice of the left in the student newspaper. Mina wrote think pieces suggesting that any money spent on the space program was bread taken from the mouths of starving children. In her most famous editorial she volunteered to be bused to a black high school if any black high school wanted to take her up on it. After graduation Mina would become a civil rights attorney in Boston, a visiting professor at Wesleyan, a collaborator with Ralph Nader, Barney Frank, and Elizabeth Warren, as well as a regular guest on *The Rachel Maddow Show*. She would be West Beth High's most famous graduate, unless Peter had dreamed the whole thing.

His gaze moved to a mumbling Ricky DeVille kneeling on the small stage, screwing together a drum kit next to a Fender Twin amplifier. Apparently, there was going to be music at this rap session. A skeletal figure came out of the wings and switched on the amp. He wore a beat-up black suit jacket over a white T-shirt and pipe-cleaner jeans. His hair was greased up in a heroic pompadour that descended into knife-edge black sideburns and a waterfall of long hair curling over the collar behind.

Peter knew it was Ricky's older brother Rocky DeVille. Not the DeVille who asked for a reward for accidently turning himself in when he dialed the TIP Line instead of the PIT Line—that was Barry. Barry was a hood. Rocky was a mondo, a slick greaser built like an open jackknife. If Peter's memory of life after 1970 wasn't a fantasy, he knew a half dozen local rumors about Rocky's eventual fate—from incarceration at the state prison to fugitive status in the Maritimes to having been found chopped up in a barrel under the Newport Bridge. Whatever cruel destiny awaited Rocky in the years to come, in 1970 he was in the small auditorium, plugging in a hollow-body Gretsch electric guitar while his younger brother, Ricky, tightened the tension rods on the drums.

Moe Mosspaw entered the room in a hurry. He was carrying a folder of papers and was dressed in his usual uniform of short-sleeve dress shirt, fat necktie, horn-rimmed glasses, and double-knit pants. He called the room to order.

"You guys in the back? Find a seat. There's plenty of places up here. Okay, we in? Everyone in? I'm not going to take attendance."

Daphne was studying Rocky DeVille with a scrutiny that made Peter jealous. He was immediately angry with himself. The DeVilles finished arranging their instruments and crouched on the side of the stage like two suspects trying to not be picked out of a lineup.

The guidance counselor spoke: "Okay, you all know what happened yesterday in Ohio. Four protestors shot by National Guardsmen during a demonstration against the American incursion into Cambodia."

"It's not an incursion," one of the black armbands shouted. "It's an illegal invasion of a neutral country in violation of international law!"

A hockey player raised his voice: "The Viet Cong are already in there! They cross the border, strike at our troops, and then run back into Cambodia, and we're not supposed to follow them? We can't win the war if we're not allowed to retaliate against attacks!"

"We have no legal reason to be there in the first place," Mina Habib said. "We've already dragged one country into a brutal war, and now instead of pulling out as they promised, Nixon and Kissinger are moving the conflict into another."

The hockey player shot back, "Nixon didn't start this war. The Democrats did, the liberals did! Nixon's trying to get us out of there with honor . . ."

The word *honor* brought hoots and jeers from the black armband crowd. Peter saw that the hockey player represented a silent majority of student council members, athletes, and class officers. They hadn't come to this meeting to man the ramparts. The treasurer of the junior class, a girl with a green vest and a white turtleneck, said, "The communists attacked the south. Would you let them just take over?"

Mr. Mosspaw tried to restore order. "Okay, gang," he said. "Good points on both sides! Now here's the thing. We won't settle the Vietnam War at this meeting. That's up to the diplomats at the Paris peace talks. Let's talk about how we feel about the deaths at Kent State. Who here wants to start?"

"Cancel final exams!" one sophomore said. His buddies giggled.

Mina Habib knew why she had come. She said, "I want our school—students and administration—to petition the governor to lower all flags to half-mast and institute a day of mourning for the slain students, and also to demand that the state legislature condemn the actions of the Ohio National Guard and ask for a full investigation of the shooting by an impartial team of prosecutors with power of subpoena at the federal level."

"Good idea," the hockey player said. "Federal prosecutors often take orders from high school assemblies."

Half the room laughed at this while the radicals looked like they were ready to bust out the machetes. Mr. Mosspaw said, "Let's hear from some other voices. Delores, you have something to read?"

Peter hadn't noticed earnest Delores of the pinioned smiley faces at the back of the room. Of course she was there—she was everywhere. She marched forward with determination, mounted the steps to the stage past the DeVille boys, and planted herself behind a microphone on a stand. She read from a poem she had composed for the occasion called "The Flower or the Sword."

I see the line of stony faces
The bayonets fixed and trained
The ideals of a generation
Falling like spring rain
Who are these child soldiers
No older than the ones they face
They can't afford to go to college
Which of us would take their place?

The reaction was an unspoken "Huh?" Moe Mosspaw clapped enthusiastically, and some of the gathering were polite enough to join in. Delores accepted her applause stoically and returned to the back of the room.

Mr. Mosspaw said, "Now Rick DeVille has prepared a musical statement about how he and, I'm sure, many of the rest of you feel about the turmoil our nation is going through."

Sharp, thin Rocky sat at the drums while Ricky strapped on the Gretsch and turned the volume knobs. Rocky counted off, and the two of them launched into a startlingly loud and off-key rendition of "The Star-Spangled Banner" in the napalm style Jimi Hendrix had popularized at Woodstock the summer before—newly available on triple LP. As few had ever heard

Ricky DeVille speak, let alone stand in front of a class, the room was astonished to see him bending the guitar strings to summon bazooka blasts of distortion at a volume that sent them across not only the small auditorium but also West Beth Vets rafters from the gymnasium to the distant G wing.

Ricky was ascending to the rocket's red glare when the door flew open and science teacher Houlihan steamed into the room, his face crimson, his belly cannonballing before him, and his fists ready to fly at the source of this sacrilege. Ricky had his head down and his eyes closed—he didn't see the torpedo approaching. Houlihan flew up onto the stage and yanked the plug out of the amplifier.

The volume went dead. Ricky opened his eyes, confused. Brother Rocky kept drumming for seven bars before he realized he was doing a solo. Seeing Rocky, a delinquent he thought he had disposed of years earlier, shattered whatever was left of Houlihan's equilibrium.

"This meeting is over!" Houlihan shouted. "You children get back to your classes! And take off those armbands! Anyone wearing a black armband in school will be suspended!"

Peter wondered if there was going to be another student massacre right there in the small auditorium. Mina Habib was shouting, "Fascism! Fascism!" and the hockey player had deputized both his goalies and the president of the student council to charge the radicals. Daphne was licking her lips in anticipation of a fistfight.

Peter took it in. He looked at the two DeVille brothers stranded on the stage with their guitar and drums and studied the melee breaking out all around him, and he stared at Daphne's profile and made a decision to surrender to his delusion. He wove between the shouting factions and climbed up on the stage and said to Ricky, "Can I borrow your guitar for a minute?"

Ricky looked like it was no weirder to him than anything else going on that day. He handed Peter the Gretsch with great care. Peter turned to Rocky and said, "Moderate march, like this," and tapped a rhythm. He hauled over the microphone into which Delores had declaimed her poem. Mr. Houlihan was waving a ruler around in the air like a saber and shouting about sending for the state police, and Mina was yelling back at him, "The whole world is watching," which was demonstrably untrue. No one in the room was paying any attention to Peter. Mr. Mosspaw restrained Mina from jumping onto Houlihan's back while the jocks and radicals ducked and weaved and dared each other to take the first swing.

Peter said into the microphone, "I'd like to express something about how we feel."

One person noticed him. Daphne. He looked at her and drew in a breath. The frets felt awkward under his fingers. It didn't matter. He could play "Ohio." He could sing it too, in an imitation of Neil Young's high and shaky voice.

"Tin soldiers and Nixon coming, we're finally on our own . . ."

Bad boy Rocky DeVille fell in behind him. The room turned his way.

By the time he got to the end, repeating, "Four dead in Ohio," every eye in the auditorium was on him. The hockey players were dumbfounded, the student council members were nodding their heads in time, Mr. Mosspaw was looking on in wonder, and Mina and the black armband boys were chanting right along, their fists in the air.

Daphne was more impressed than if Peter had pierced his nipples with paper clips and stuck a pencil in his eye.

Vice Principal Lockwood, former Peace Corps volunteer and almost-nun, had arrived to stop a riot and found herself instead standing in the doorway with tears on her cheeks.

The last chorus of “Ohio” faded. Peter let the echo of the final chord ring. Teachers and students who had crowded into the room to see what all the noise was clapped and whistled. Ricky and Rocky DeVille slapped him on the shoulder and told him he was great.

“Peter,” Mr. Mosspaw asked, “you wrote that?”

“Yes sir,” the boy said.

The guidance counselor said, “I had no idea you were so talented.”

Peter smiled and took in the applause. He said, “Wait till you hear my song ‘Stairway to Heaven.’”

# TEN

On Saturday morning Peter stretched out on his bed, considering that he had performed "Ohio" in public before Neil Young had written it. The bad news was, when the Crosby, Stills, Nash & Young version came out in a few weeks, he would be exposed as a plagiarist. The good news was, when the CSNY version came out, it would be proof that he knew the future.

He was listening to the plastic clock radio on his nightstand. He heard the Moments, Melanie, Tyrone Davis, and the Jackson 5. It pleased him that in 1970 rock and roll still meant black and white music together. It would be another few years before FM radio consultants would resegregate the genre and "rock and roll" would come to mean white boys with guitars only—as if Little Richard and Fats Domino had never happened. As if Ray Charles and Chuck Berry had not invented the form.

His mother called from downstairs that Dr. Terry was coming up the driveway on his motorcycle. The radio said, "Here's a big WPRO exclusive! It's the new track from the Beatles! Those reports of a breakup were premature. Here's the latest from John, Paul, George, and Ringo—'So Intoxifying.' The Beatles on PRO!"

Peter stared at the radio. It was playing a Beatles record he had never heard. A darting McCartney bassline bounced off Ringo's rolling drums, and John Lennon's unmistakable voice rang out with a lyric about feeling like he had his fix every time we kiss.

Peter said, "This is impossible."

He let the song finish and listened to the disc jockey talk about sticking around because in the next half hour he would play the flip side. "The Beatles are back, and we've got 'em on the station that reaches the beaches—WPRO!"

He wandered downstairs into the library where Dr. Terry was waiting.

"Here's the songwriter," the therapist announced when he saw Peter. "The hero of the protest rally! It's a thin line between madness and creativity, Pete."

Peter was distant. He said, "Doctor, something very strange just happened. I heard a new song by the Beatles on the radio."

"Not an unusual occurrence, Pete."

The boy rubbed his forehead. "No, it's impossible. The Beatles broke up in April of 1970. Everybody knows that. Paul sued the other three to dissolve the partnership. They never got back together."

The doctor became serious. He said, "That's how it was in your experience? In the delusion?"

Peter nodded.

The doctor said, "So how do you reconcile this new song?"

Peter said, "The disc jockey was playing a hoax. It's Badfinger. It's Klaatu."

"Pete, I got something to show you. You see today's paper?" Dr. Terry opened his leather satchel and pulled out the *Boston Globe*. He pointed to page one. Peter looked at the headline. He said, "That can't be."

Dr. Terry read the headline out loud: "Rockefeller Dies in Plane Crash."

Peter said, "It's wrong. Nelson Rockefeller becomes vice president after Nixon . . ."

Terry said, "After Nixon resigns, right. That's what you said. Turn on the news." The doctor read from the paper: "New York governor Nelson Rockefeller died in a plane crash in Pennsylvania last night. Also killed were the pilot of Rockefeller's Learjet and one of the governor's aides."

The doctor passed the newspaper to the boy.

"Pete, the world you think you remember . . ."

Peter's face went from puzzled to distraught. The doctor said, "The Beatles are not breaking up, Pete. Nelson Rockefeller is not going to be vice president. I very much doubt Richard Nixon is going to resign. And you could not have stopped the Kent State massacre, because as hard as this is to accept, you did not know it was going to happen."

He waited for Peter to respond. He didn't expect him to say, "I have to make a phone call."

Dr. Terry followed Peter into the front hall. He was asking the operator for directory information for Long Beach, New York. He asked for the phone number of a Mr. Gus Crowley on Sawchuk Road.

Dr. Terry watched as Peter protested. He hung up and tried again. He argued. He put down the phone and stood facing away from the psychiatrist.

"They said there's no Gus Crowley in Long Beach, and no Sawchuk Road."

"Who is Gus Crowley?" the doctor asked.

"My father-in-law. My wife, Janice, grew up on Sawchuk Road in Long Beach, Long Island. Her dad built the house right after the war. In 1970 he would have been an undercover narcotics detective. By the time I met him he was chief of police. Imagine that, huh?"

"Peter . . ."

The boy was shaking. "How could that not be true?" He began to sob, and Terry Canyon reached out to him. "Doctor, how could none of my life be true?"

"Remember what we talked about, Peter? You can love your wife and children as a memory the way you loved your parents before you got them back."

Peter said, "But they never existed? I'm supposed to accept that they never existed?"

In the kitchen Peter's parents were drinking iced tea.

Joanne said, "He seemed good today."

Howard said, "He's strong, Joanne. The doctor says he's exceptionally bright."

Joanne said that she wondered if that pretty girl would come around again. Howard said there would be time enough for that. Peter was only fifteen. He asked if she had spoken to their daughters. Cathy was newly married in Rochester. Sally had moved with a boyfriend to Vermont. The parents had told them nothing about their little brother's trouble.

Joanne said, "Do you think we didn't pay enough attention to Peter? With the girls we were so involved."

"The girls were demanding," Howard replied.

"Peter was always easy."

"My old man used to say, when the first kid drops a cookie on the floor, you grab it and throw it away and give him a new one. When the second kid drops a cookie, you pick it up and wipe it off and hand it back to him. By the third kid, you say, 'Pick up that damn cookie and eat it!'"

She had heard that story a hundred times.

They watched the clock and sipped their drinks until they heard the door close behind the doctor. Peter wandered into the kitchen and opened the refrigerator. He leaned in, moving the cartons and bottles, and said, "Mom, whole milk again? Bacon, processed ham, and Miracle Whip. We have to start eating healthier."

His mother said, "I spoke to Dr. Sullivan. He agrees that whole milk, eggs, and plenty of red meat is the best diet."

Peter said, "Dr. Sullivan smokes Old Golds while he examines his patients. He dies of a massive stroke my first year of college."

He shut the refrigerator and turned around. His parents saw that he had been crying.

"Are you okay, Pete?" Howard asked.

"Rough session," Peter said.

"If you'd like to try a more traditional counselor . . ." Joanne offered.

"Terry is great," Peter said. "This is just some shit . . . sorry, Mom. This is just some stuff I have to go through. It'll be fine."

His mother looked unconvinced. His father said, "As long as he's not trying any of that orgone box, primal scream baloney . . ."

"Not at all," Peter said. He sat at the kitchen table between his parents and peeled an orange.

"School going okay?" Joanne asked.

"I got elected to be a student representative to a special assembly."

His parents were cautiously encouraged. Joanne said, "How did that go?"

"It went well," Peter said, taking a bite of his orange and talking with his mouth full. "I actually got up and sang a song I wrote. It got a big reaction."

The parents were surprised. Howard said, "I guess that old guitar of yours is paying off. Maybe you'll play some dances."

"Maybe," Peter said. He had a strange expression. His eyes were shining but his voice was even. "It turns out I'm a gifted songwriter. I wrote a song called 'Ohio' about Kent State. After I finish my homework I'm going to start writing *Game of Thrones.*"

Peter's parents exchanged glances. Joanne asked if the boy wanted her to make him a hamburger.

"Mom," Peter said, "I'm going to make you a deal. You stop eating poison, and I'll stop acting like a crazy person and we'll get back to normal. Green vegetables, fruit. We can eat fish, we can eat some chicken. Please. I don't want to lose you."

Joanne considered how to respond to that. She put her hand on her son's neck and said, "Fair enough, Peter. We're in this together."

Peter threw his arms around her. She was startled but didn't resist. She hugged him back.

He said, "Mother, you're all I have left."

# ELEVEN

> As I headed deeper into mists and old stories, into windy images poised on the rim of sleep, I began to feel that the bed was having a dream and that the dream was me.
>
> —Don DeLillo, *Great Jones Street*

For three days Peter refused to get out of bed. He wouldn't come downstairs to speak with Dr. Terry. He wouldn't get up for school. The only foods he would eat were Hydrox cookies and Waleeco bars, which he explained to his parents would no longer exist in 2020. "I'm trying to find something positive about being here," he said, and then turned off the bedroom light.

At 7:00 a.m. on the fourth day, Moe Mosspaw appeared at the front door. To the amazement of the boy's parents, Peter came downstairs fully dressed, as if nothing was wrong. He took a bite from a banana and accepted the guidance counselor's offer of a lift to school.

On the ride, Mosspaw asked where he had been. Peter said he had been sick. The counselor asked, "With what?" Peter said, "The bends."

Peter got through the morning counting the heresies. The man who taught history said that Africans allowed themselves to be enslaved but Indians were too proud. The woman who taught English wouldn't accept that the word *where* in the sentence "I saw in the paper where Judy got married" could be grammatically correct.

In algebra class Mr. Wood welcomed the head of the math department, who talked to the students about the importance of learning the metric system. He told them that by 1990 the United States would be on the metric standard and anyone who still thought in inches, miles, ounces, and pounds would be unable to hold a job.

Daphne passed him a note. "I want to ride your horse."

Peter folded the paper in quarters and nodded toward her without making eye contact. Daphne would have to get into her own trouble, without help from Peter Wyatt. He had troubles of his own.

Mr. Houlihan sat behind his mayonnaise-stained blotter and read aloud from the science textbook. Peter stared at the clock, begging it to tick another minute. He decided his first theory had been right—he must be in a coma. This was the last illuminated corner of his mind to which consciousness fled as the lights flickered out. Another half hour of hearing about vacuoles and he wouldn't mind going.

At fourth lunch, Peter was waylaid by Ricky DeVille carrying a plate of American chop suey.

"Wyatt, I got to talk to you," Ricky said in his low monotone. He guided Peter toward the last table in the lunchroom, domain of greasers, hitters, and voc-tech short-timers. An overweight kid with a failed mustache slid over to give them room.

"That song about Ohio," Ricky DeVille said. "You write that?"

"Yeah," Peter said, "It just kind of came to me." Hedging his bets, he added, "I might have been channeling Neil Young."

"That's cool," Ricky said. "My brothers and me have a band, you know. Malleable Iron. We played out at the lake last summer, at the Barge, and we played the Youth Club in New Greenwich, the coffeehouse at St. Gregg's. You ever hear us?"

"No, sorry."

"Because the thing is, we really want to get into doing some original material. But in our style, you know? We do some Blue Cheer, Doors, we do 'Heartbreaker' by Grand Funk. A lot of Steppenwolf—that's kind of what we're known for mainly. We do 'Monster,' we do 'The Pusher' for, like, twenty minutes. There's a manager from New York who's come to see us a couple of times, and he likes us but says we got to write our own stuff. My brother says we need a big anthem like our own 'Born to Be Wild.' You got any ideas for a song like that, like 'Born to Be Wild'? A Hells Angels kind of song?"

Peter said, "How about 'Born to Run'?"

Ricky's hair was draped over his tinted aviator glasses. He sang the words "born to run" over the melody to "Born to Be Wild" and then said, "Like that?"

Peter said, "Not really. Picture eighth notes like a motor on the bass strings of a Telecaster, okay? Like duh duh duh duh duh duh duh duh duh." He slapped the corner of the table. "Now think of a big Roy Orbison voice with Phil Spector echo and he's going, 'In the day we sweat it out on the streets . . .'"

Peter talk/sang the lyrics to "Born to Run" in a low voice. Ricky had his head down, his focus on the table. Even as he laid it out, Peter was aware that his version sounded like a sequel to “Eve of Destruction” arranged for accompaniment by a manual typewriter and sung by Mister Ed. When he finished, Ricky raised his eyes and said, “You just came up with that right now?”

“I had some of it already.”

“Can you write that down for me?”

When Peter finished writing out the lyrics, lunch was over and he hadn’t eaten. He grabbed a ham loaf on white bread and a four-cent carton of milk and was wolfing it down when his childhood friend John North caught up with him. Peter felt guilty. He had been avoiding John since he woke up in 1970. He didn’t want to let him in on his secret, and he was pretty sure he couldn’t pass for the teenage buddy John was accustomed to hanging around with.

Puberty had not yet found John North. He had a high voice, the smooth cheeks of a child, and fine, fair hair. He said, “Everybody’s talking about your song.”

“Crazy, huh?” Peter replied.

“You’re hanging out with Ricky DeVille?”

“Did you know he and his brother have a band?”

“I thought his brother was in Socko.”

“He has a couple of brothers.”

“Barry DeVille was pretty scary. When we were kids he killed Mrs. Quigly’s cat.”

“I don’t know if that was ever proved, John.”

“Mrs. Quigly opened her door and her cat was hanging from the porch fan. She fainted right there. My father had to take her to the hospital and then come back and cut down the cat.”

"I do remember that."

"Be careful around those guys."

"I will."

"I kept in touch with John North," Peter told Dr. Terry at the next session. "He's one person from 1970 who was still in my life when I left 2020. Sweet guy. Worked as a carpenter in Hartford until he hurt his back. I had lunch with him around Thanksgiving. I got the impression he was stretched financially. I remember he said the bad thing about being in your sixties is you don't know how much money you need for the future. If you're going to live to be ninety, you have to keep working. If you're going to die in five years, you'd rather quit now and see the pyramids. Mathematically, either outcome is equally likely. Of course, by the time you find out the age at which you're going to die, it's too late to make any plans."

"Everybody dies too soon," Dr. Terry said.

"Not objectively," Peter answered. "But from their own perspective, certainly."

"When you look around your school, you feel like you know everybody's destiny?"

"No," Peter said. "Most people I don't remember, and I don't know what became of most of those I do. But some, yeah. There's a guidance counselor named Maurice Mosspaw. He ran the Kent State meeting."

There was no reason for Dr. Terry to let on that he had met with Mosspaw.

Peter said, "When we were kids, I think we made fun of him. But I looked at Mosspaw at that assembly and saw an earnest man doing his best to herd hundreds of uninterested adolescents through a system institutionally indifferent to their needs or potential. He hectors them to sign up for the SATs, apply for scholarships, and engage in after-school activities to impress admissions officers. He writes letters of recommendation, chaperones school dances, supervises field trips, and serves as faculty advisor to a half dozen student clubs. As I recall, Mr. Mosspaw died of AIDS in the eighties. He couldn't have been older than fifty." The boy stared at his knee and said, "I wish I had made time to go to his funeral."

Dr. Terry said, "What's AIDS?"

On the school bus the next morning Peter tried to pick out the students who had died before 2020. He saw a baseball player named Keith who would pile up his car on the night of the senior prom. He wondered if he should warn him. But that would just be taken as further evidence of his lunacy. And perhaps that was all it was.

# TWELVE

Ricky DeVille lived within walking distance of the high school, in a ranch house across from a small strip mall at the far corner of the parking lot of a large A&P grocery store.

There were three businesses in the strip mall—a pharmacy, a liquor store, and a Greek diner. Ricky suggested that they stop at the diner and pick up a couple of wieners before heading to his house to rock out. They bought their hot dogs and stood in the parking lot chewing them. Ricky directed Peter's attention to three matching fluorescent signs hanging over the doors of the three businesses: DRUGS, LIQUOR, WIENERS.

"The three major nutritional groups," he said.

Peter had assumed that the DeVille brothers were poor, but their house and yard suggested they either had money once and lost it or still had money and were slobs. The place needed painting, there was a beat-up Plymouth Barracuda sitting on blocks in the driveway, and a couple of tires lay sprawled on the overgrown lawn. When they walked around back, the boy was surprised to find a large swimming pool. It was empty except for an outboard motor someone had deposited in two feet of rainwater in the deep end. There was a bent-legged trampoline, a motorcycle half covered by a yellow tarp, and a homemade skateboard ramp so treacherous it might have killed Evel Knievel. Two dirt bikes leaned against the outside wall of the freestanding shed, which served as the DeVille brothers' music room.

They had a lot of expensive gear. It was not impossible that the DeVilles stole it, but it occurred to Peter that the family might have more money than he had guessed. In mid-twentieth-century America there wasn't much connection between income and class. It was the golden hour of union jobs and domestic manufacturing.

The biggest surprise was Ricky's mom, who came out of the house and told Peter it was nice to meet him. He had expected the mother of three notorious tough guys, the oldest of whom had to be at least twenty-one, to be either a hardened Ma Barker type or the sort of down-beaten bad-luck wife in photos from the Great Depression. Mrs. DeVille was nothing of the sort. She was no older than forty and tall. She had tinted blond hair, a broad smile, and a figure not far past what must have been a traffic-stopping heyday.

To be attracted to the mother of one of his classmates excited Peter and then embarrassed him.

Mrs. DeVille told the boys to have fun and try not to make too much noise. Then she jumped into a silver MG two-seater and peeled out.

"What does your dad do, Rick?" Peter asked.

Ricky DeVille said, "He's not around."

The rehearsal shed was as big as a small garage. The drum kit and amplifier from the Kent State assembly were set up, along with a couple of microphones, a small Peavey public address system, two other amps, and several guitars. There was an old upholstered couch along one wall and a dilapidated upright piano with chipped keys against the other. The decorations were a mix of black-light posters—Hendrix loomed large—and pinups from girlie magazines. Peter did a double take when he thought one of the posters was of the DeVilles' mom. He was relieved, on inspection, to see it was Barbarella.

Ricky suggested Peter choose a guitar, and he selected a half-decent Stratocaster knockoff made by Sears. He plugged it in, Ricky turned on his Gretsch, and they began to riff on "White Room" until the door opened and switchblade-shaped Rocky walked in, followed by older brother Barry, the jailbird juvenile delinquent and suspected cat killer.

Ricky and Peter stopped playing. Barry nodded for them to continue and dropped onto the couch. Rocky took a seat behind the drums and began tapping out a beat.

Barry DeVille was shorter than his brothers, but there was no question he was the dominant primate. He had broad shoulders, a tiny waist, and stumpy, muscular legs that he squeezed into jeans two sizes too small. He wore his hair in an anachronistic pompadour that recalled Michael Landon when he was a teenage werewolf. Where middle-brother Rocky's ice-cool greaser pose suggested a self-consciously retro fashion statement, Barry looked like someone who had been locked up since 1963 and didn't know styles had changed.

Barry spread his feet far apart. He had a can of Narragansett beer in his hand. He said, "This is the kid?" His brothers nodded. Barry said, "What's your name?"

"Wyatt. Pete Wyatt."

"Okay, Pete Wyatt, play me a song you wrote your own self."

The boy went into "Ohio"—his hit—while Ricky and Rocky rumbled along in and out of key and tempo. When it was over Barry swigged his beer and said, "What else you wrote?"

Peter said, "Here's an idea I'm working on," and launched into "Sweet Home Alabama," still four years away from being written by Lynyrd Skynyrd. He was giving it his all until he opened his eyes and saw Barry waving for him to stop.

"I don't think that's a hit," he said. "You got something better?"

Peter didn't think he could pull off David Bowie's "Heroes," and he was pretty sure Barry would hate U2's "I Still Haven't Found What I'm Looking For" as much in 1970 as he probably did when he heard it through the bars of a penitentiary in 1987. He tried "We Are the Champions" and Barry stopped him again.

"That's not even rock," he said.

"Okay," Peter said. "This will rock you."

He laid into the riff every kid walking into every music store plays when he picks up a guitar he cannot afford. Peter hit the DeVille brothers with "Smoke on the Water." This time he was allowed to play the whole song. When he finished, Ricky said, "That's cool," and repeated the riff a few times on his Gretsch. Rocky nodded.

Barry said, "I don't like the words, though." What else?

Peter played "Every Breath You Take" and Barry said it was dumb.

He played "Money" by Pink Floyd, and Barry made an elaborate yawn and fanned his face.

Peter hit him with "Blitzkrieg Bop," and Barry said, "Now that's just stupid. Your songs are getting worse."

Frustrated, Peter asked, "Why are we doing this? Are we putting together a band or what?"

Ricky said, "Barry knows that guy in the music business."

Peter said, "So?"

"So," Barry said, jumping from the couch and getting close enough that Peter could smell the beer on his breath, "this guy Lou Pitano is a big-time agent and record producer. He's gotten bands signed to Buddah Records, okay? You know that song 'The Last Surfer'? Louie Pitano cowrote that and produced it."

Peter said, "Wasn't that in, like, 1962?"

"So you do remember it!" Barry cackled as though he had just proven intelligent design. "Lou's mother comes from around here, and after all his success in New York City he's back in town looking for local talent to sign to publishing, production, and recording deals. I brought him to hear my brothers and he said he liked the sound . . ."

This alone was enough to make the boy question the A&R credentials of Lou Pitano.

"But he said we need original songs. Now, I worked on that thing you gave Ricky, 'Velvet Rim.'"

"It's called 'Born to Run,'" Peter said.

"Not anymore. We fixed it up; we improved it to the point where I would consider submitting it to Lou. But we can't walk in there with one song. We need at least four. So I'm looking at you and asking, Do you have any songs that are good enough to impress a professional music executive who until recently had his own office at Kama Sutra Records?"

Peter played Barry "Little Red Corvette," "No Woman No Cry," and "Superstition." Barry didn't like any of them. He finally got his attention with "School's Out" by Alice Cooper.

Barry thought that had potential. Around this time Ricky and Rocky traded instruments, Ricky going to the drums and Rocky to guitar.

Trying to think like a DeVille, Peter pulled out "Smokin' in the Boys' Room," which would be a hit in 1973 for Brownsville Station if the boy didn't get to it first, and if Brownsville Station were other than a figment of his elaborate imagination.

When he finished, Barry paced up and down for forty seconds before turning to the ragged combo and saying, "Now *that* is a fucking song!"

Ricky and Rocky laughed and whooped. Peter was overwhelmed with gratitude that he had finally hit Barry DeVille's level. Barry made them play "Smokin' in the Boys' Room" four more times. The last time he produced a cheap office cassette recorder with a built-in microphone and held it in front of Peter's face and said he would now record a demo for the great Pitano.

"Wait," Peter said. "Hold on. Barry, you're not going to get anything but noise out of taping the song on that toy. I assume going into a professional studio isn't an option? Okay, if you want to get this . . . talent scout to hear our music, he's going to have to come down here and let us play for him live."

Ricky and Rocky murmured agreement, and Barry didn't immediately veto the idea. Peter pressed on: "But not yet. Look, we're not a band—we've never even played together before. The best thing we can do is pick three songs and really rehearse the shit out of them until we have them right, and then get this guy over to hear them. I mean, if he doesn't like what he hears the first time, I'm guessing he won't be back."

Barry nodded. Peter said, "We have to talk about arrangements, too. Do you guys own a bass?"

Ricky said he knew where they could get one. The boy did not want to know what that meant.

When he recounted all this to Dr. Terry, the therapist asked why he was suddenly investing so much energy in starting a rock band.

Peter took a moment to gather his answer.

"I have considered the possibility that I'm not going to wake up out of this alternative reality tomorrow or the next day or this year. With every hour this world feels more real and the life I've lived for the last fifty years seems more abstract. I keep repeating to myself the names of my in-laws, my coworkers, my poker buddies. I keep going over family vacations, my children's teachers, their birthdates—anything to stay tethered to who I really am and the life I've lived. What if the longer I stay in 1970, the more I lose of the future—my past?"

"Is that what you feel is happening?" Dr. Terry asked.

Peter plowed on. "If this huckster who Barry DeVille knows has any connection to the music business at all, I might be able to use him to get me to someone who would recognize the value in the catalogs of Billy Joel, the Eagles, and—let's not piss around—Michael Jackson. Elton John hasn't written 'Candle in the Wind' yet. I'll start with that. 'My Heart Will Go On'? That has to be worth a thousand dollars."

"These are songs you wrote?" Dr. Terry said.

"These are songs I'm going to write," Peter said. "I figure it's a win-win. Either Neil Young and Elton John and Brownsville Station show up with the same songs and I prove I'm from the future, or they never write them and I get rich."

Dr. Terry said it was good that Peter was engaging with positive aspects of being in 1970.

"If I'm going to be forced to live my life over, I'm going to do everything the second time that I wish I had done the first time," Peter said. "And that starts with making a million dollars before I get to eleventh grade."

Dr. Terry scratched his neck and said, "You comfortable fixing that ambition to the DeVille brothers?"

"Shit, Doc, I've been around the music business for forty-five years. I've lived through 'Disco Duck,' Black Oak Arkansas, and Sebastian Bach. The DeVille brothers are sophisticates by comparison."

# THIRTEEN

Daphne Burrows bought twelve dollars' worth of windowpane acid from Rocky DeVille and proposed that Pasa meet her at the supermarket so they could try it out. It was the climax of an entire school year of speculating, theorizing, and debating when and where they should initiate their relationship with LSD. They had studied paperbacks about it, burned incense in Pasa's rec room, listened to Ravi Shankar records in preparation, and bought black-light posters at Spencer Gifts. There was a great bridge between intention and commission, however, which was finally crossed when Daphne approached the middle DeVille after the Kent State assembly and asked if he would help her score. Rocky came through behind the A&P, which Daphne decided would be a good place to trip.

"Why the supermarket?" Pasa wanted to know. "Shouldn't we go to the ocean? Trip on the beach? Or the zoo. We could take the bus to the zoo and look at those little monkeys with the long tails."

Daphne thought Pasa was stalling. "I'm not going to go all

the way to the zoo on acid," Daphne insisted. "Let's take it right now and go inside. It will be crazy. The soup cans will look like they were painted by Andy Warhol."

Pasa kept arguing for the ocean, but Daphne put her foot down. She opened the envelope Rocky had sold her and took out a small square of paper and popped it in her mouth.

"Daphne!"

"I'm going into the A&P. Are you coming?"

"Daphne! Maybe we should go to your house."

"And have my mother see me with pinwheel eyes? I don't think so. You want to take yours?"

Pasa was having trouble making the leap from the theoretical to the actual. "I'm going to wait and see if you need any help or anything."

"*Cluck, cluck*—chicken!"

The two girls entered the market cautiously. Piped-in music was playing. Daphne said, "That melody is so weird!"

Pasa was concerned. "It's 'Tiny Bubbles,' Daphne. It's not weird."

"It sounds like it's under water. Oh wow—look at that freaky bald guy. He has an earring!"

"That's Mr. Clean. It's a cardboard cutout. Daphne, it's only been, like, five minutes. I don't think it should be working yet."

"My senses are super acute. I can hear your heart beating."

"How about if we go to my house? My mom's not home. We could go to the rec room and turn on the TV with the sound down and play records . . ."

"I went to Peter Wyatt's house," Daphne told Pasa. "We fed his horse, and he took me up to a spooky hayloft. We kind of made out."

Pasa was horrified. "He could have killed you with a pitchfork, Daphne! He could have attacked you."

"Do you think he's cute?" Daphne asked.

"I think he's a psycho."

Daphne smiled. "He told me he's been to Mexico and Morocco."

"He's a lunatic."

Daphne whispered, "He told me he's married."

Pasa said, "That freak is going to hurt somebody, Daphne. My mother says a whole group of the parents are going to make sure he's taken out of school."

Daphne twirled around in the aisle staring at the fluorescent lights in the ceiling. She said, "I'd like to go to Morocco." She extended her hands into the air and walked delicately down the cereal aisle like Ophelia. Pasa followed.

A deep male voice seemed to come out of the air around them. It called their names. Pasa was certain it was the police. Daphne smiled and wandered toward the sound.

Moe Mosspaw said, "Hello, girls! Hunting for bargains?"

Pasa was confused that the guidance counselor was dressed in a white butcher's apron, plastic gloves, and a little cardboard beanie. Daphne stared at him with open-mouthed wonder, hoping he was her first hallucination.

"I work part-time in the meat department," Mr. Mosspaw announced. "It's really a summer job, but I do every other Saturday during the school year to stay on the books."

Pasa nodded. She wished Daphne would at least close her mouth.

Mosspaw said, "You okay, Daphne?"

Daphne stared into Mosspaw's eyeglasses and said, "One of your irises is bigger than the other."

Mosspaw said, "That's right. Childhood accident. My brother was chasing me and I tripped, and a coat hanger went into my eye. A little piece of it is still in there. See?"

He leaned forward, lifting his glasses so Daphne could get a good look at his pupil. Daphne tipped toward him with beatific delight. She said, "A little speck of metal floating in an ocean of green."

Pasa told Daphne they had to go and said so long to Mr. Mosspaw in his cardboard hat.

"He's a *teacher*, Daphne," she whispered as she led her psychedelicized friend out of the store by the arm.

"Ivory Snow," Daphne said as if it were a secret. "Ivory Snow. Ivory. Snow."

They crossed the parking lot and Pasa tried to steer Daphne in the direction of Pasa's house, but Daphne wasn't having it. She stepped into the road and stuck out her thumb.

Pasa said, "What are you doing? You can't hitch a ride—you're too fucked up. Come to my house!"

A beat-up Mustang convertible blasting Rare Earth slammed to a halt and slid onto the lip of the road in front of the two girls. A skinny guy with a bent nose and a drooping mustache looked back at them from the driver's seat and said, "Wherever you're going, jump in."

Pasa tried to pull Daphne toward the curb, but Daphne yanked away from her and climbed into the passenger's seat. Pasa made a muted angry noise and hauled herself into the small jump seat, a crevice behind the driver.

"My name is Slocum," the driver said. He was wearing a pea-green army surplus coat and had mirrored sunglasses pushed up on top of his head. "Sam Slocum. What's your names?"

Daphne was smiling and studying her hand. Pasa said sadly, "This is Gidget, and I'm Larue."

"Where you ladies heading?"

"Across town," Daphne said without looking away from her fingers. "That farm on the hill on East Shore Road."

Pasa kicked the back of Daphne's seat.

Sam Slocum said, "Isn't that where the judge lives? I don't like that man. He sent a good friend of mine away."

"My boyfriend is his son," Daphne said. "He has a horse."

Sam Slocum said, "What if we drove out to the reservoir? I got a buddy with some good grass."

Pasa said, "No thanks."

Daphne said, "Does your buddy have a horse?"

The Mustang made it to the bottom of Peter Wyatt's driveway in the time it took to hear two-thirds of the album version of "Get Ready." Sam Slocum stopped at the foot of the road and put his car in park. He said, "I don't want to go up there, but I'll wait here for you if you think you might want to head to the reservoir after you look at the pony."

"Okay," Daphne told him.

Pasa climbed out of the jump seat and said, "You shouldn't wait."

Sam Slocum said, "How old is she, anyway?"

"Fourteen."

"See you later."

Daphne wandered up the road to the Wyatts' house with Pasa suffering along behind.

They went to the kitchen door and Daphne cupped her hands around her eyes and leaned against the screen, peering inside. She said, "Oh. Hi, Mrs. Wyatt. Is Peter home?"

Pasa was hanging back, ready to make a run for it. The door opened and the boy's mother was there, smiling.

"Daphne, nice to see you again." She looked at Pasa. "Hello."

"This is Pasa," Daphne said. "I was telling her about your horse. Is Peter here?"

"Peter is at rehearsal in Buttongreen," the mother said. "He and some other boys have a little band."

This was big news to Daphne. "Gee, we just came from Buttongreen," she said. "Who was he rehearsing with?"

"I think the boy's name is Rick."

"Ricky DeVille?"

"That sounds right."

"Okay. Thank you, Mrs. Wyatt."

Daphne led Pasa back down the long driveway to the main road, where she stuck out her thumb once more.

"I can't believe Peter is right now playing music on the other side of town with the brother of the boy we bought this acid from."

Pasa said, "Let's call my mother and ask her to come pick us up."

Daphne said, "Look, Eleanor, if you're not going to take that other hit, fork it over. I'm coming down too soon."

# FOURTEEN

What kind of music industry mogul would go into a tool shed in a suburb sixty miles from Boston to listen to a teenage band that had never played a paying gig? Lou Pitano was that sort of mogul. A skinny little man in his late forties wearing pressed jeans and a shiny leather jacket, his protruding eyes darted left and right behind tinted prescription glasses while a small ring of white glue peeked out from the prow of a toupee that almost matched the color of what remained of his hair.

Lou spoke with a broad Brooklyn accent of the sort that would no longer be heard in 2020 and might have been an affectation in 1970. Lou explained to Peter and the three DeVilles that after enjoying great success in the New York City record business, he had relocated to New England in search of fresh talent.

"I had an office at Atlantic Records," Lou declared. "A skyscraper. Bert Berns, Jerry Ragovoy, I knew 'em all. If a light bulb blew out in my office, I was not allowed to fix it! I rang for building services and they sent a guy up to change the bulb for me."

The DeVilles' mouths were open in admiration.

"But New York is fished out. The Rascals, Tommy James, all the great acts are taken, and there's nobody good coming up."

"You work with the Velvet Underground at Atlantic?" Peter asked.

"That sort of crap is why I got out. If they're signing shit like that, time to move to fresh water. See, everybody else has headed to California. What? Am I going to be one of a hundred schmucks trying to find the next Sonny and Cher? No, I come here—because where nobody else is looking, that's where the new thing appears!"

"Okay!" said Ricky DeVille.

"So you boys, you got some songs?"

"We do, sir," Barry said. Rocky flashed astonishment at the "sir."

"Let's hear them."

They launched into "Smokin' in the Boys' Room." They weren't as tight as Peter would have liked, but it was a hard song to mess up. His fifteen-year-old voice was an instrument of neither strength nor beauty, but Peter knew enough to not oversing. "Smokin' in the Boys' Room" was a story told in the voice of a teenager caught with cigarettes in the school lavatory. An adolescent yowl was compatible with the subject matter.

They collided to a stop and studied Lou Pitano's expression. He gave away nothing. He said, "What else ya got?"

They had "School's Out" by Alice Cooper. This composition stretched the talents of the ensemble to the peak of their competence. Peter turned to the DeVilles to steer them through the tricky "No more pencils, no more books" passage, and by the time they got to the last triumphant chorus, Lou Pitano was moving his right foot as if he were doing the twist from the waist down.

"That's not too bad," he announced to everyone. He said to Peter, "You wrote those songs?"

Peter nodded. Lou Pitano reached into the pocket of his jacket and withdrew a transistor radio. He clicked it on and began spinning through the stations.

"I want to play you cats something," he said. Through the static they heard bits of "Venus," "ABC," and "Thank You (Falettinme Be Mice Elf Agin)" before the mogul smiled and let the dial come to rest on "Love Grows (Where My Rosemary Goes)." He held up the radio. The DeVilles were impassive. The mogul said, "You boys know this song?"

"Yeah," Ricky said like he was giving a deposition to a hostile attorney.

"Okay, now hang on," Lou insisted. He fiddled with the transistor some more. Snatches of "Give Me Just a Little More Time" and "Ma Belle Amie" went past. He was searching for something. The boys had no idea what to say, so they said nothing.

It took stops at the news, weather, and "No Sugar Tonight" before Lou found what he was looking for and held the radio in the air in victory. It was "Gimme Dat Ding" by the Pipkins, as stupid a novelty song as ever got airplay.

"You know this?" the mogul cried.

"Yeah," said Rocky. "I know it blows."

Lou Pitano turned off the radio. "Oh, you think it blows, do ya?" he said. "Uh-huh. And how about 'My Baby Loves Lovin'' by White Plains. Do you think that blows, too?"

"Pretty much," Rocky admitted. The DeVilles' awe of the mogul was rubbing up against their instinctive contempt for authority figures. Rocky was measuring the contrasting rewards of continuing to be deferential to Lou versus pantsing him and peeling off his hairpiece.

Lou the mogul was reaching his thesis: "What would you teenage experts say if I told you that 'Gimme Dat Ding' by the Pipkins, 'My Baby Loves Lovin'' by White Plains, 'Love Grows (Where My Rosemary Goes)' by Edison Lighthouse, and by the way 'United We Stand' by the Brotherhood of Man were all in reality the same singer recording under four different names?"

"I'd say somebody better shoot that motherfucker," Rocky replied.

"It's true!" Mogul Lou said triumphantly. "What I'm telling you is completely confidential and known to only a handful of music-industry insiders. All four of those groups don't really exist! There's a producer in London who puts these records together and uses session musicians and a singer named Tony something and they put band names on them and look at what he's done—he's got four big international hits at the same time, and nobody knows there *is* no White Plains, there *are* no Pipkins, there's no such *place* as Edison Lighthouse!"

Now Peter spoke up. "Sounds like a really good deal for the producer. Not so great for Tony Something, the singer with four big hits and nobody knows who he is. Think it's safe to guess that Tony Something was paid a flat fee for his services and isn't seeing any royalties."

Lou looked at Peter as if he had just presented DNA evidence that the mogul's mother was a donkey. He said, "What are you, Jack—a lawyer? I happen to know that Tony the singer is driving around London in a new Porsche with a famous miniskirt model. Tony is doing just fine, thank you. Now, what I envision is a similar production setup for myself and my company right here in this vicinity. I plan to pay for studio time for a number of young musicians and singers to come in and record tracks that I'll use my connections to place with major record labels and for which I expect to sustain national radio airplay. Are you gentlemen interested in being part of such a project?"

"Yeah," Ricky said.

"Yes," Rocky said.

Peter said, "What's the financial arrangement?"

For one second Lou the mogul looked like he wanted to attack Peter's throat with a can opener. Then he smiled and said, "How much cash investment do you want to contribute? I'm paying for the studio, I'm absorbing all the costs, and I'm the one with connections in the record and radio world that are virtually priceless."

Peter began to say that in the music business, "priceless" often turned out to be "worthless," but he held his tongue. Lou said, "And you boys are contributing what?"

"The songs," Peter said. "That little thing."

"I have not heard a song here today," Lou said gravely, "that has the lyrical depth of 'United We Stand' or the melodic sophisticatedness of 'Love Grows.' You got a song like that?"

"Yeah, I got a song like that," Peter said. He took a deep breath and hurled himself into Leonard Cohen's "Hallelujah."

When he got to the end, Lou smirked and said, "You got a guy tied to a chair and a chick taking a bath on the roof. I don't know what you were smoking when you wrote that, kid, but do me a favor and don't get behind the wheel. Anything else?"

Peter hated the little creep. He sang him the cheesiest song he could think of: "Billy Don't Be a Hero" by Paper Lace.

When it ended, Lou Pitano's eyes darted behind his glasses, and the tip of a lizard tongue shot out and swept his thin lips. He shouted, "That's a hit! I'll give you two hundred bucks for that song, right now!"

"Five hundred," Peter said, "for half the publishing for six months. You place it by Christmas, you get to keep your half. Otherwise it reverts to me. And I keep the whole writer's share."

"Kid," the mogul said, "that ain't how this business works."

"Sure it is, Lou," Peter told him. "I got a subscription to *Billboard*."

The DeVilles were confused, leaning toward hostile. The mogul was supposed to have come to discover their band. Now Peter was making his own deals in legal language they didn't understand. Not wanting to be disloyal or get punched in the eye, Peter told Lou the Mogul, "I want to cut the band in on the writer's share. Ten percent for each of them." He turned to the DeVilles and said, "Where I go, you guys go with me."

Lou Pitano shrugged like he figured if the kid was stupid enough to give away thirty percent of his royalties to three goons in a shed, there would be plenty of future opportunities to outsmart him.

"Now, Mr. Pitano," Peter said, "you think we can make a date for the band here to get into your studio and record 'School's Out' and 'Smokin' in the Boys' Room'?"

"I get a producer's fee!" the mogul declared. "That's standard industry procedure."

"We coproduce," Peter told him. "The band gets paid four hundred bucks for the session at the session. After that we'll all waive our fees until the money comes in, at which point producers' fees, musicians' royalties, and publishing will be dispersed at the same time. We get paid when you get paid."

Lou Pitano's face hardened. Whatever really drove him out of New York—and it wasn't the hunt for fresh talent in the provinces—was in the back of his eyes. He hadn't come to the sticks to be dicked by a fifteen-year-old kid. If Peter wasn't careful, Lou's greed for his songs would be overrun by a pride that had already taken a lot of kicks. He said, "You think you know how the business works, huh, kid?"

Peter downshifted. He said, "I don't know as much as I'd like to, Mr. Pitano. I'm anxious to learn what you can teach me."

Mogul Lou didn't trust the sudden display of respect, but it allowed him to back off from telling Peter to take his little songs and blow them out his ass. He said, "I'll record your songs, but—no offense, kid—you ain't a professional singer. You stick to the guitar, and I'll bring in a vocalist radio could play."

Ricky DeVille finally had something to say: "Let's get the guy who did 'Gimme Dat Ding.' That dipshit will sing anything."

# FIFTEEN

"What do you know about reincarnation, Dr. Canyon?"

The psychiatrist lit up. "Samsara! The wheel of existence. Part of Buddhism, Hinduism, Jainism. The Greek philosophers discussed the transmigration of souls. The Celts and the Persians. Belief in reincarnation is common to cultures and religions across history and on all populated continents. In Central America I spent a lot of time—"

Peter stopped the doctor before he could recount his mind journeys with the Yucatec.

"Suppose reincarnation exists, but we have it wrong."

"There's a rule book?"

"Suppose we don't go from body to body. Suppose we reenter our own bodies over and over."

"Life on a loop."

"Right. When we die, we rewind and begin again. Only maybe we don't necessarily rewind all the way. Maybe with each incarnation we start over at the point where we fucked up. Over a thousand lifetimes we have a shot at eventually getting it right all the way through."

"And then what? On to Valhalla?"

"I have no idea. Maybe at that point you become a cow."

"How did you land on this theory?"

"I'm trying to figure out what's happened to me. I'm entertaining all ideas because, let's face it, the reality I'm living through is more ridiculous than any explanation I could come up with."

"You're back in 1970 to fix something you did wrong the first time?"

"Maybe. Maybe there was a screwup. Maybe I wasn't supposed to remember my last fifty years. Some cosmic quality control officer was asleep at the conveyor belt and put me back here without erasing my memory of 1970 to 2020."

Peter studied the doctor, who was searching for an appropriate response. Peter said, "It sounds far-fetched when I say it out loud."

"No, no," said Terry. "Any system that helps you reckon with your delusion and move forward is worth exploring. Look out the window. Up and down this street are intelligent, educated people who pray to Yahweh that their kid gets into prep school and light candles for the souls of the faithful departed. I have people I went to Harvard with who camp on ley lines and praise Gaea. Whatever floats your ark, man."

"Is it off-limits to ask what you believe, Dr. Canyon?"

"It's all in the mind, kid."

There was a knock on the office door. Protocol was being breached. The doctor got up, annoyed. His assistant apologized for breaking in. She said the hour was up, Mrs. Wyatt was outside, and she knew the doctor and Peter would both want to hear what was on the news.

The Vietnam War was over. Nixon's invasion of Cambodia had worked. Faced with America extending the combat across Indochina, the Russians and Chinese had pressured the North Vietnamese and Viet Cong to accept Kissinger's peace plan. A formal cessation of hostilities and recognition of the 1965 borders by both sides would be signed in Paris in three days. North and South Vietnam agreed to hold free, multiparty UN-monitored elections within ten months. It was May 19, 1970, and the war was over.

The doctor whooped and hugged his assistant.

"Hate to see those fuckers get the Nobel Peace Prize," he said, "but whatever gets us out of there . . ."

He looked at Peter, who was pale.

"Not how you remembered it," the doctor said.

"No. It didn't happen this way where I came from."

The doctor said, "This is better, though, right?"

"I suppose it is."

The doctor motioned to his assistant to leave them and close the door.

"Peter, I want you to consider that maybe this world you woke up in is an improvement over the one you left. The Beatles are still together. The Vietnam War is over. You have your whole life ahead of you, knowing all kinds of stuff other people don't figure out until they're too old to do anything with the information. Don't think of your being here as a malady to be cured. Try to think of it as a blessing."

"My wife."

"Maybe she'll still come into your life, man. Maybe you'll find her in twenty years on a journey down the Nile. Maybe when you're thirty you'll see the name of her band in a newspaper and live that part of your life over again. Don't waste the second youth you've been given worrying about things you can't control that won't happen for years anyway. I don't understand what happened to you, Peter, but I know you're greatly gifted. Maybe what we've been calling a delusion is the biggest gift of all. Grab it." He gathered his papers and walked to the door and added, "Show the universe some gratitude."

"'Ooh La La,'" Peter said.

"What?"

"'I wish that I knew what I know now, when I was younger.' It's another great song waiting for me to write it."

The doctor asked if the boy had any idea what he did wrong last time that he had been sent back to correct.

"I've been going over that," Peter said. "My life worked out well. I have no regrets, at least no regrets from high school." He stopped and stared at the wall. The doctor let him come around.

"One thing I did always feel was a missed chance. I mean, when I was a teenager. It was nothing really. In the scheme of a whole life it was nothing."

"Spit it out, kid."

"Did I mention Amy Blessen to you already?"

"Remind me."

"She was the most beautiful girl. Partly because she didn't know she was beautiful. She wasn't a cheerleader type. She was an athlete. What we used to call a jockette—she played on all the girls' sports teams. A lot of boys were intimidated by that because she could sink a basket and mount the parallel bars and hit a softball better than they could. And I think she was self-conscious about not being girly. Anyhow, I was crazy about her."

The doctor asked Peter if he'd ever dated her.

"Anytime I was around her, I got flustered and said something stupid. Then, toward the end of tenth grade, spring of 1971, I heard her talking to her friends by the lockers. Her family was going to move to the next town during the summer. Instead of my having two years to figure out a way to get her to go out with me, I had four weeks."

Dr. Terry said, "You say this girl is shy and doesn't have a lot of boyfriends. Why don't you just go up to her and say, 'Hey, Amy—want to see a movie?'"

Peter reacted like the psychiatrist was a slow learner.

"Well of course I would do that *now*. As a grown man. I would have done that if I had known her when I was twenty or twenty-five or thirty or anytime I had some experience with women. But this girl paralyzed me. I'd projected all my adolescent desires onto her. If she came up to me and smiled, I got so self-conscious I walked away."

"Where are we going with this, Peter?"

"Spring of 1971. I'm sixteen. I start forcing myself to say hello to her every day."

"You're a regular Robert Wagner."

"She's so sweet! She always smiles. We start talking almost every day. She tells me about the girls' track team and how in the summer she sails a little sunfish around the bay and she asks if it's true I have horses. This fantasy girl I've been staring at for two years is becoming someone I can really talk to."

The doctor slid his vision to the wooden clock on the shelf behind the boy's head. They were way into overtime.

"So it's June 1971. It's the last day of final exams. Now, I should explain that by that time my mother had gotten a new car and I was driving her old station wagon. I'd installed an eight-track and put some Grateful Dead skull stickers and a Rolling Stones tongue on the bumper. I was fully loaded."

"What's a Rolling Stones tongue?"

"It's coming soon. So this is the last day of school. Kids are roaming the halls in cutoffs and flip-flops. The teachers have given up caring about anything but getting out for the summer. Everybody's loose and happy. John North comes up to me, dragging along this skinny girl with crossed eyes and no bra and says, 'Hey, let's drive down to the beach, Alice has some Zest Tabs.' I say, 'No, man, I have an English final.' He says, 'Blow it off, you got the car.' I say I can't do that, but of course it's not really about the English final—it's about my last shot with Amy Blessen. I can see John North is frantic to be with this girl, so I hand him my car keys and say 'Bring it back to my house before suppertime' and he splits. I don't care about anything but seeing Amy.

"I get to the classroom and get a seat next to Amy and we take our exams, and it's English, it's easy, we both finish early. Pretty soon every kid in the class has turned in the exam and someone asks if we can go. Our teacher is a real ball buster and she says, 'No, we all stay in this room until the final bell rings.' Which is about thirty minutes away. All the other kids groan but I'm so happy because it gives me half an hour with Amy. And she's in a great mood; she's telling me about all her plans for the summer and asking about what I'm doing and where I'll be over vacation, and we're really talking and I figure maybe I can work the conversation around to my going to see Taj Mahal in the park next week and hey, maybe she wants to come, and then—it's like she's looking straight into my brain—she says, 'Gee, I'm supposed to be back here at three thirty for our final girls' volleyball game and I have to go home first and there's no way I can make it all the way to my house and back here in half an hour. I don't know what I'm going to do.'

"Doctor, time stopped. Everything froze in place, and I realized that this is the moment I've been waiting for all year. Amy needs a ride. And I have a car. I will politely offer to drive her home, I will meet her mom, I will sit in her living room drinking a ginger ale while she grabs her stuff, and then we will drive back to the school together and she will thank me and I will say, 'Hey, Amy—why don't you come over to my house this weekend and we'll go horseback riding.'

"My whole future is laid out in front of me. I've scored the goal at the bell. After the last class we will ever have together, I'm going to give Amy Blessen a ride home.

"Except . . . I gave my car keys to John North, and right now he's parked at the beach getting stroked by cross-eyed Alice. I have no car. I cannot offer Amy a ride. All I can do is look at her stupidly and say, 'Well, good luck with that.'"

Peter looked like he was recounting the fall of Troy.

"And then the bell rang and we went in opposite directions for the rest of our lives."

The doctor took a moment to be sure the monologue had ended. He said, "Let's break down this story."

Peter said, "In 2020 they would say 'Let's unpack it.'"

"Why would they say that?"

"I don't know, Doctor. In the future they charge double for any shit labeled 'bespoke,' too. People take pictures of their dinners and text them to their friends. Things are strange in the future."

"It's getting a little goofy in the present here, too, Pete. I hate to ask, but—does Amy Blessen exist in this reality? The one outside my window?"

"Oh yeah, she's playing freshman field hockey. I saw her the day before yesterday."

"Well, why don't you ask her to the dance, man?"

"What dance?"

"I don't know what dance—the Spring Fling, the Freshman Frolic. Ask her to come over and swim in your duck pond."

"Doctor, you have an optimism I would call charming if it didn't suggest your having lost all sense of context. I'm the crazy kid, remember? I'm the loon who took his clothes off in class. This is not the moment for me to spring a rendezvous on a fourteen-year-old girl who has at this point never been on a date, never been kissed, and certainly would be horrified to be approached by the school lunatic. No, I have to get certified sane by you, let a year go by, ease back into the adolescent flow, get my driver's license, do push-ups for a solid twelve months, clear up my complexion, grow sideburns, reconstruct my slow approach to Amy Blessen, and—most essential—tell John North he can't borrow my car on the last day of tenth grade so when Amy needs a ride home I'm there with keys in hand."

The doctor said, "Peter, I'm very happy you have goals in this reality, and Amy sounds like a terrific girl. I think you're wise to take things slowly. She *is* only fourteen."

"Right—and I was married for thirty-five years and have grown children."

"You might want to hold off laying that on her. But," the doctor said, "it's good that you're being positive about the upside of being a healthy fifteen-year-old with your whole life ahead of you. That's progress."

Peter became reflective. "I miss my wife and children terribly, Doctor. It's hard to accept that they weren't real. In a way, it's worse than if they'd died. To behave as if they'd never lived . . ."

Shit, he was slipping again. The doctor mumbled something sympathetic.

Peter closed his eyes and steadied himself. He was silent for a long time. Then he said, "Did you know I can go twelve hours without having to pee?"

The doctor told him, "Fate giveth, and Fate taketh away."

The boy said, "Fate has made of me a yo-yo."

# SIXTEEN

Peter took a bus across town for band rehearsal. When he got to Buttongreen, there was no sign of any DeVille brother in the rehearsal shed. He waited awhile, strumming a guitar. He tried to work out the chords to a Steely Dan song. After half an hour he gave up and walked past the empty swimming pool to the back of the house and knocked on the kitchen door. Mrs. DeVille came and opened it. She was wearing a sleeveless turtleneck with a small rip at the collar, black Capri pants, and no shoes. Her toenails were bright red. Peter saw that she had beautiful toes.

"Hi, Peter."

"The boys around, Mrs. DeVille? We were supposed to practice."

"Oh, honey, their daddy showed up unexpectedly. Only way he ever shows up. Rocky and Ricky went with him and their little brothers to the drag races."

"There are more brothers?"

"Their daddy has two little boys with his new wife. She has a twelve-year-old, too."

"Jeez, they're like the Osmonds."

"Yes, well, Ricky and Rocky did me a favor, getting them all out of here. Raymond and I can stand to see each other for about nine minutes before one of us forgets to pretend to be civil. It's good they see their father, though."

"Okay. Well, tell them I came by."

"You want to come in for a Coke, honey?"

He stepped into the kitchen, and Mrs. DeVille went to the refrigerator and came out with a Tab. She asked if that was okay and Peter said yes, and she poured it into a glass and handed it to him.

She said, "I'm glad you're friends with Ricky, Peter. He's more sensitive than he lets on, and he's very smart. In first grade his teacher told me his IQ test said Ricky was gifted. Don't tell him I told you that."

"He's a smart guy," Peter agreed. He couldn't get over how pretty Ricky's mother was and how awkward that made him feel.

"I'm glad to see him making friends with a nice boy like you, a boy from a good home. A nice family." She was looking into the middle distance. "All I wanted for my boys was to have a good home life, a solid upbringing. Raymond and I got married so young. But, you know. If we hadn't, I wouldn't have Barry . . ."

"I think," Peter said, "that successful marriages are impossible to predict. A husband and wife need to be about fifty-five percent identical and forty-five percent compatible opposites."

Ricky DeVille's mother looked at Peter with curiosity. "What does that mean, honey? Compatible opposites?"

"Maybe the husband is good at making money but bad at hanging on to it. The wife is his compatible opposite—she keeps the books, pays the taxes, and keeps the operation solvent. Maybe he's impatient and she's always late. She teaches him to relax, and he gets her to church on time."

"You are a very wise young man. Did you learn this from your parents?"

Peter couldn't say he'd learned it from thirty-five years of marriage, so he gave his mother and father credit. He knew he should shut up, but he liked the way she looked at him—impressed.

"It might sound stupid," Peter said, "but I think in every successful romantic relationship, one person is the cop and the other the crook. The crook drinks too much at the dinner party and the cop drives home. The crook forgets to do the Christmas shopping but the cop has it all wrapped up. In a really good marriage, the two people swap playing the cop and crook. Two cops and you have no fun. Two crooks is chaos. Two people switching back and forth makes for a solid marriage."

Ricky DeVille's mom stared at Peter. There were little lines under her large green eyes.

"You're how old, Peter?"

"Fifteen."

"Ricky says you write wonderful songs. He speaks highly of you."

"Thank you."

"Will you play me a song you wrote?"

Peter began to say he didn't have a guitar. She walked into the next room and came back with a nylon-string acoustic. He took it and tuned it and leaned against the sink. What to play for the abandoned first wife with the red toenails and the wounded eyes?

He sang "Buckets of Rain," which Bob Dylan wouldn't record until 1975. When he finished, Mrs. DeVille looked at him as if he'd appeared with the Virgin Mary in a circle of flame.

"Honey," she said, "you wrote that song all by yourself?"

"I guess so."

"Oh my God. Play me another."

He said, "You don't have a piano, do you?" and she said yes, there was a spinet in the living room. They went to it and he sat with his back to her and found the chords and sang Springsteen's "Racing in the Street," a song about failed dreams and faded glory. He knew what he was doing. When he got to the line "wrinkles around my baby's eyes and she cries herself to sleep," she let out a little gasp. He let the last chord ring and then took a moment before turning to look at her. Her eyes were wet.

"I don't know how a boy your age could know those things."

"I just do."

"Ricky told me about how you got in trouble . . ." She waited to see from his expression if it was okay to bring up the scandal. He nodded. "Why did you do that, Peter?" and then, in a whisper, "Take off your clothes like that?"

"I'm not sure I can explain it," Peter said. "I think I wanted to do something that would make everything change. I wanted to turn the chessboard over. If I did something I could never take back, at least it would get me out of the way things were. Have you ever felt like that, Mrs. DeVille?"

"Two times," she said. "Once when I wasn't much older than you are now and I ran off and married the boys' daddy."

"When was the second time?"

"Every day since."

They watched each other.

She said, "I'm glad you're friends with my boys, Peter. You're a good influence on them. Ricky is special, but he doesn't believe he is. His father was never a good example. Barry tried to be strong, and you see where that led . . . Every time his daddy shows up Barry disappears. I might not see him for a week now."

"How come you never remarried?"

Mrs. DeVille blushed. She said, "A thirty-eight-year-old woman with three rowdy boys . . ."

"But you're so beautiful . . ." Peter was surprised it came out. He watched it land.

She looked at her feet, at those perfect toes and nails painted red, for who? For nobody. She said, "Well, aren't you sweet to say so." She stood. "I have to go to the A&P in case their daddy forgets to feed them."

She looked straight at him, and the boy got the message. He drained the rest of his soda and thanked her for the drink.

She said, "Thank you for the concert, Peter," and took his glass and went into the kitchen and washed it. He waited a minute after he heard her turn off the tap, and when she didn't come back into the living room he called out, "Okay, then. Thanks, Mrs. DeVille. Bye."

He left by the living room door. It was a big surprise, he thought, to find someone else in 1970 who was as stranded as he was.

# SEVENTEEN

Dr. Terry spent Sunday morning in his hammock rereading all his notes on Peter Wyatt. He had a new idea.

"I've been treating Peter the adolescent," he wrote in his leather journal. "What would happen if I tried treating Peter the sixty-five-year-old man?"

At their next session the analyst asked Peter what had been going on in his life in the weeks before he woke up in 1970. Did he have any big problems, any pressing worries in his life in 2020?

"Christmas shopping. I always ended up doing all the Christmas shopping for our kids, Janice's siblings, my sisters' families. I was way behind. I remember thinking there should be a cutoff for having to buy gifts for nieces and nephews once they get out of college and are self-supporting, but Janice insisted we get something for everyone, and she could never decide what. She'd go to the mall for five hours and come out with a pair of couch pillows. It always fell to me, and I remember thinking I was out of time and had no ideas."

Dr. Terry said that if that was his greatest source of anxiety, Peter was living a very lucky life. The psychiatrist tried steering the boy toward deeper water. “You told me that the tough thing about being over sixty was that you didn’t know if you should plan on living five more years or thirty. Were you losing a lot of friends, Pete?”

“Not losing,” Peter said cautiously. He stopped talking for a full minute before he said, “You get to know so many people in a lifetime—it seemed like every month we heard about someone else getting sick.”

Dr. Terry waited.

Peter swallowed. “Remember the kid in the high school play who tried to pass for an old man by putting talcum powder in his hair? That’s who I saw in the mirror every morning. For thirty years I kept saying, ‘Pipe down in there,’ ‘Leave your little brother alone,’ and ‘Turn out the lights and go to sleep,’ until one night the house was as empty as a ballpark in November and I had the quiet I’d asked for. And I didn’t want it.”

“Tell me who was sick,” the doctor said.

Peter struggled. “Everybody was getting cancer. Cancer of the throat, cancer of the esophagus, prostate cancer in the men, breast cancer in the women. They went for radiation and chemo and surgery and got worse and then got better. They went back to their jobs and lives but now with shadows in their eyes that suggested they’d looked over into the abyss and couldn’t forget what waited for them. Janice told me she felt like we were being surrounded by illness.”

The doctor nodded. Peter continued.

“A buddy of mine, a *Rolling Stone* writer named Charlie, learned he had a brain tumor. They operated. When he woke up they told him, ‘We got most of it.’ You don’t want to hear ‘most’ in those circumstances. Charlie never married. He had no family.

He took the news with a good humor I could hardly comprehend. He made jokes about how having brain cancer wasn't as bad as having to go on the road with the Sex Pistols. One day we were walking back from his chemotherapy. He was leaning on me. He said, 'Pete, I have a scheme. You know my apartment is rent-controlled.' I said okay. Charlie said, 'This being Manhattan, I've already had a couple of discreet inquiries about whether I'd consider willing the apartment to someone in exchange for a nice cash payment immediately.' I said, 'You're not serious,' and Charlie said, 'Cancer brings out the best in people. Two different acquaintances have gently suggested they would pay me big money today to add their names to my lease so that when I expire, they can assume residency.' I said wow, and Charlie told me he was thinking of taking them up on it. I said, 'You're not,' and he said, 'Yes, I am, but here's the hook: I'm going to sell my posthumous lease to ten or fifteen different schnooks for ten grand each. I can bank at least a hundred thousand dollars, and by the time any of them find out about it I'll be dead! What could possibly go wrong?' I said, 'You could go into remission.' Charlie said, 'Shit, Pete, you're right. Wouldn't that be my luck?'"

Peter looked at Dr. Terry. They both smiled. The psychiatrist gestured for the boy to keep talking.

"After Charlie died I continued to get up and go to work and to the gym and watch TV, but I found myself slipping out of time. One summer evening I was walking down the street toward my house carrying a grocery bag and I thought, 'I used to live around here.' Where did that come from? I still lived there.

"More and more often I experienced . . . not melancholy, but a sort of gentle displacement. Like the light was changing and time was falling away. It felt familiar somehow; I had known this before. I finally placed it. It was the feeling I used to get as a kid in late August when summer vacation was running out. Only now it wasn't summer fading—it was my life. The long days never felt sweeter than they did as they escaped.

"In my dreams the years started bleeding into each other. I would be driving along in the car with my kids in the back when they were little and my mother as she was when I was a child in the seat next to me. Fifty years ago and ten years ago and yesterday afternoon jumbled together. I had dreams in which I was in our apartment in Tribeca and when I opened the closet door I found myself in my childhood bedroom. It was like the old days of reel-to-reel tapes where you would record over a song but still hear an echo of it playing under the new track.

"I started to look forward to falling asleep. I liked seeing my parents again. I enjoyed spending time with my children when they were small. I knew I was dreaming, but that didn't make it any less fun. Until the day I drifted off in my swimming pool in 2020 and woke up here, with roosters crowing and my father alive and telling me to get out of bed before breakfast got cold."

Dr. Terry pushed his chair back. He swung around and hauled open a drawer in a table and pulled out a pocket-size notebook. He tossed it to Peter.

"I told you before to write down big events. Now I want you to write down memories of your life in the future. Trips you took. Arguments with your wife. Stories about your kids. I don't need to see what you write, but I'd be interested to hear you talk about what comes up."

Peter asked what he was thinking.

"First thing they teach you in shrink school, buddy. Never tell the patient what you're thinking."

"What are they gonna do, Terry? Take back your diploma? I told you everything that's going to happen for the next fifty years. It's only fair you tell me what's going through that head of yours."

Dr. Terry said, "It's not a formed opinion. It just occurs to me that maybe on some level you wanted to be fifteen again. It's a safe refuge."

They stared at each other.

"Bingo," Peter said. "Terry, you cracked the case. Can I go home to 2020 now?"

"I don't know, Pete. You certain you really want to?"

# EIGHTEEN

Peter's mother sat at a long library table with a yellow pad in front of her. On either side of the pad were stacks of books. She had pages marked with slips of paper. She had a red pen and a green pen in front of her and a black pen in her hand.

A thin woman with a Mia Farrow haircut approached her and said, "Joanne? Joanne, how are you?"

Joanne Wyatt looked up and ran through a roll call of moms from Peter's grammar school PTA. She clicked on the right name.

"Dorothy, hi. What brings you to the stacks?"

"Returning overdue books. I found two volumes of Tolkien in Eleanor's closet and a copy of *The Harrad Experiment* checked out at Christmas under her bed."

"How is Eleanor? All As?"

"She wants everybody to call her Pasa now. I think it's something to do with sympathy for Cesar Chavez." Dorothy's face turned from amusement to concern. "How is Peter?"

Joanne's throat clenched. She was the mother of the crazy boy. "He's doing very well. Thank you for asking."

Dorothy tried to sneak a casual look at the books Joanne was reading. She said, "Biological science. Not my best subject."

"I'm doing research for an article. Academic journal. Boring stuff."

"You never stop, do you, Joanne? A doctorate, three kids. Everything you have to deal with . . ."

Joanne thought there might be an accusation in that. Why was she working on an article when her child was having a public breakdown? She told herself she was being oversensitive. Dorothy didn't have the depth to be duplicitous.

"Say hi to Eleanor for me. Or Pasa, if she prefers."

"I will. And give my best to Howard. And Peter, of course."

Joanne smiled and nodded and went back to her work. She had a new schedule. Each evening after she filled the dishwasher with the dinner plates, she came to the library for an hour to do research on possible explanations for Peter's condition.

Last week she had dug deep into Jung and Nietzsche's writings on *amor fati* and the Eternal Return—the theory that energy recurs in similar forms across time and space. Eternal Returners believe that all of nature operates on a loop with slight variations. It could explain Peter's dilemma. There could have been a crossed wire between two cycling lives, and her son had picked up the memories of a parallel Peter.

Eternal recurrence had been part of the science of civilizations through recorded history, from Egypt to India to the Pythagoreans. "You can't dismiss Pythagoras," she thought. "His math still checks out."

She had completed her notes on the Eternal Return and moved on this week to biology and consciousness. She was studying how learning is passed down genetically, how animals inherit information through a process we don't understand and that we dismiss with the limiting word *instinct*.

She felt her husband approaching. She knew his footfalls and his shadow before he put his hand on her shoulder.

"Joanne," he said softly. "You have to come home. They want to close."

She looked around the room. Where had everyone gone?

Howard Wyatt sat down next to her. "You learn anything?"

She tore off four pages of notes and folded them in half. She wrote on the back, *Reverse transfer?*

Her husband looked at her with kindness.

Joanne said, "Howard, I've been working through an idea. Consider this: We don't understand what consciousness is. We don't. We don't know what causes it or where it ends. We look at the brain and we say, 'That's where consciousness lives.' But that's a primitive proposition. Really, it's like saying love resides in the heart. All we know about consciousness is that it seems to parallel electrical activity in the brain—but it's a rough correspondence at best. It's not much better than measuring fate by the stars."

"Joanne, if you start doing Peter's astrological chart, we're getting a divorce."

She smiled. "All I'm saying is, we don't actually know where consciousness resides or how it moves. We know it somehow nests in the brain, but no one knows how much of the brain it occupies. There are many cases of patients with severe head injuries finding skills attributed to the disrupted part of the brain manifesting elsewhere. A soldier loses the sphere that controls speech, and in a few months speech appears again, having migrated to a healthy part of the brain."

Howard sat back in his chair. He nodded. He was making the same focused but unreadable face he wore in court when listening to testimony.

Joanne said, "Let me put it this way. A metaphor."

"You're teaching in parables now?"

"Imagine a species from beyond our galaxy looking through a giant telescope at us. They have no bodies; they're made of gas. They're compiling a record of life-forms in the Milky Way. They train their sights on Earth. Never heard of the place. They zoom in on New York City. What have we here? This planet seems to be populated by great concrete creatures, immobile and a thousand feet high. When the sun goes down, these creatures light up. They're awake. They're communicating with one another along electric lines. As the night proceeds, their lights go out; they're asleep. Next morning they begin to operate again. Thousands of tiny little creatures are drawn into them and expelled out. That must be their food source. They suck these little bugs in and shit them out again.

"Now, it would never occur to these intergalactic census takers that the microbes going in and out are actually the ones with the consciousness. They would never suppose that the buildings, the lights, the power grid, the entire organized progress of the city is being run by the tiny bugs, not the concrete giants."

Howard considered this. He said finally, "Well, we certainly have put one over on those alien gas creatures."

Joanne touched his arm. "It's a metaphor. Howard, we look at the brain the way they look at the buildings. They assume the consciousness resides in the entire structure, but what if it doesn't? What if consciousness is cellular? What if it's microscopic? It could be. It could be that all we think and know resides in a cell within our brain. And if that were true, Howard—what if consciousness is migratory? When the body dies, the conscious cell might move through the soil into a plant or tree. It might migrate through the earth."

"Honey, we're not Druids."

"Howard, what if consciousness is actually hereditary? Why would that be any stranger than inheriting your father's ears or your mother's eyes? And what if somehow, in Peter's case, a consciousness that was supposed to be moving forward through time somehow reversed course? What if Peter isn't an old man who came back in time but a fifteen-year-old boy who has been fed a preview of his next fifty years?"

Joanne looked at her husband with an expression that was almost desperate. She wanted so much for him to comprehend what she was proposing. He didn't have to accept it. He just had to comprehend.

All she got back was unwelcome sympathy.

He said, "We'll never know, and it's a waste of time guessing. Joanne, I know you want to believe in Peter. I know you want to support him. But he doesn't need you validating his delusion or vanishing down tunnels toward the unknowable. He doesn't need you to come up with arcane theories to justify his fantasy."

Her face flushed. He knew he was on shaky ground. She was smarter than he was and could dismantle him in any debate, even if he was right and she was wrong. Especially if he was right and she was wrong. He knew that from experience.

Judge Howard Wyatt leaned toward Dr. Joanne Wyatt and whispered, "Our boy needs his mother to be at home and to know she loves him. That's what Peter needs."

The lights were clicking on and off. The library was closed. Joanne pulled the marked sheets out of the books on the table and put her papers into a large leather bag. She walked out of the building with her husband following her.

She put the key in the door of her car and waved to him.

He thought, "We can't afford to lose her, too."

She thought, "He never was good in a crisis."

# NINETEEN

Nothing could murder Peter's faith in public education like health class. The teacher—a beefy former college football player with curly hair and a jutting chin—announced that today's subject was "Condoms, prophylactics, sheaths, or, as you've probably heard older kids refer to them, rubbers, safeties, raincoats, the fez."

He flexed his thick neck and stuck out his awning jaw.

"You guys gotta know about this stuff for when you"—here he almost snickered—"get married and consider family planning." He was bouncing a half piece of chalk in his right hand. He looked around the room for someone not paying attention. His eyes fell on a chubby kid with a pubic mustache. The young teacher reared up like he was back in the URI Thanksgiving game and winged the chalk at the kid, who snapped to attention as it cracked against his ear.

"Frisco!" the teacher barked. "What are the two main reasons for using a prophylactic?"

Frisco rubbed his ear and considered. "Because the girl won't let you do it otherwise?"

The teacher laughed. "You're a scholarship student, aren't ya? That's not a bad answer. Girls! If any of you ever in your distant future lives find yourselves in a situation where you're considering becoming intimate with someone like Frisco . . ."

A stereo-panned *Ewww* rose from the young women in the room.

"By all means, make such a course contingent on his having functioning protection. For your sake, for his sake, and for the sake of your unborn children, who we pray to God stay that way."

The boy in front of Peter raised his hand. "Mr. McCabe?"

"Yes, Rolly?"

"Ain't a rubber a waste of money? Don't most guys just use one of their socks?"

The health teacher stared at Rolly, a pimply boy with one sleepy eye, to determine if he was making a joke. Nothing but sincerity registered on Rolly's bumpy face. Mr. McCabe tried to stifle his amusement but couldn't. His lips began to quiver, someone else laughed, and pretty soon the whole room was in hysterics while Rolly looked around and said, "What?"

Peter's next class was at the far end of the school. He would have to haul ass to get there before the bell. He passed John North in the hall, who made a gesture that he wanted to talk. Peter nodded and kept moving. He turned from F wing into D wing and passed a large bulletin board, which Delores Marx had decorated with smile faces and a banner that said, "HAVE A NICE DAY!" Beneath that banner someone had tacked up a cardboard sign with an American flag and the slogan "POWS NEVER HAVE A NICE DAY." Some wiseass had come along with scissors and a stapler and moved the letters around so the sign now declared, "WOPS NEVER HAVE A NICE DAY."

Peter arrived at the Language Lab and took a seat behind a plastic screen and put on the cheap headphones. Through the static a recorded voice said, "*Bonjour. Je vais bien. Et vous?*"

The French teacher sat at the front of the classroom looking bored and clicking through switches. You never knew when he was listening to you. Peter remembered an old trick—you just moved your lips as if you were answering, and when the teacher got to you he would think the microphone was broken and move on. Peter did that for a while before he got bored.

The taped voice said, "*Comment allez-vous?*" Peter sighed and said, "*Bonjour, ma ami invisible. Je souhaîte que je pourrais dire que j'étais bien mais je me trouve dans un dilemma métaphysique. Je suis un enfant encore, emprisonné dans la Bastille de mon corps de quinze et forcé endurer le tedium d'un journée à l'école dans les printemps de 1970. Est ce qu'il y a un sant Gallic à qui je peux petition m'aider échapper et rétourner à la monde de mobiles et télévision réalité?*"

He heard a ticktock in his earpiece. The French teacher had been listening. For a moment Peter wondered if he had found a way to prove he was from the future. In 1970 he could barely conjugate *aller*. He was bringing a college education and a lifetime of European travel into the Language Lab today. He waited to hear the teacher's response.

The response was, "Ha ha, Wyatt. You go to the trouble of memorizing that whole spiel? Wouldn't it have been easier to just do the homework? Get with it."

The French teacher's voice clicked off. The static came back on. Peter went back to moving his mouth with nothing coming out.

# TWENTY

As Peter approached the rehearsal shed behind the DeVilles' house, he heard a woman doing a passable impersonation of Grace Slick. "Don't you want somebody to love?" It was not a trained voice but it was effective, on pitch and cutting through the squall of Ricky's electric guitar and Rocky's bass. Peter was curious until he got to the door. Then he was furious.

He said, "Daphne, why are you here?"

Daphne was wearing a W. C. Fields T-shirt that ended just above her navel, hip-hugger jeans, and an expression that projected *Why, whatever do you mean?*

She said into the microphone, "We're just having fun, Peter."

Rocky rested his wrists on his bass with an aplomb that was nearly Parisian. A long cigarette dangled from his lower lip. He said, "Daphne's a good singer. Lou Pitano said we needed a good singer."

Peter had no objection at all to handing over vocal duties to someone with a better voice than his own adolescent gargle. The object was to get the songs sold, not become the next

Rod Stewart. But Daphne could sabotage the project. Not only was she emotionally unprepared for the work the boy knew was ahead of them but she was a troublemaker by instinct and aptitude. She would create chaos and then stand back and enjoy watching it. The amateurism of the DeVilles and the sleaziness of Mogul Lou were obstacles enough. Daphne would harpoon the whole plan just to see the carnage.

"He didn't say a female singer," Peter said. "'Smokin' in the Boys' Room,' 'School's Out,' 'Smoke on the Water'—those have to be sung by a guy."

Daphne let the microphone slip by its cord down to the floor. She looked toward Rocky with an expression of innocent heartbreak. He reached out his long arm and pulled her close. "Oh my God," Peter thought, "she's hooked him already; the fragile-looking fourteen-year-old honor student has got the eighteen-year-old mondo under her thumb, and she's going to wreck my band."

"The Airplane has Marty and Grace," Daphne said coyly. "I don't need to sing on every song. Just once in a while."

Peter made a quick survey of the moment's politics. Rocky was clearly smitten, and Ricky would side with his brother. Barry's whereabouts were unknown since his father came to town. Peter decided to stall.

"Maybe Daphne can sing in the demo session," he said. "We can see how it works out later. Right now we have to keep rehearsing. Studio time is expensive, and I don't want us to be into Lou Pitano for more dough than we have to be. Let's work."

Daphne smiled and went and sat on the battered old couch and drank a beer conspicuously. Peter saw her batting her eyes at Rocky. "This is going to end so badly," he thought.

They rehearsed their songs for the demo session. Every pass got better. Rocky and Ricky stayed between the lines, found the pocket, kept it simple. They ran through "School's Out" six times and "Smokin' in the Boys' Room" four times, and then "School's Out" twice more. On the last pass Rocky began to vary the bass line, climbing up the neck, showing off for Daphne. Peter stopped the song.

"Rocky, you're drifting. Stick to the figure."

He said it without thinking. If Daphne weren't in the room, it wouldn't have caused a shrug. But Daphne was there, and Rocky the tough guy couldn't be corrected in front of a girl by a little rich kid.

"You worry about trying to sing, sonny," Rocky said. "I'll play the bass."

Peter wasn't going to get Rocky back on track today. Better to let it slide and get him focused again tomorrow, when Daphne would, God willing, be gone.

"I have another song we should try," Peter said. "Check this." Rocky was looking at him suspiciously, but when the boy hit the riff from "Rebel Rebel" it changed the mood in the room for the better. Ricky counted off the beat and Peter hit the chords. Rocky listened for a minute while he lit a new smoke, nodded, and fell in. Peter closed his eyes and began singing. By the second chorus he was sharing his mike with Daphne. She yelled "rebel rebel" every time it came up and hummed loudly in between. She shimmied and bopped and pressed her leg against Peter as she leaned into the microphone. She sounded pretty good. She looked pretty good, too, he thought. To which he immediately appended the certainty that such thoughts would lead to disaster.

# TWENTY-ONE

Dr. Terry Canyon was reading the *Whole Earth Catalog* when Peter came into the room. "I'd like to learn how to use a loom," the doctor said.

"A substantial investment," Peter replied.

The doctor closed the book. "Not if you make all your own clothes. Think of the long-term savings."

"You going back to the earth, Doctor?"

"We all go back to the earth eventually."

"Not me, apparently. I was preparing to journey toward the necessary end when I boomeranged back here to puberty."

The doctor gave Peter his attention. "I thought we agreed to accept the reality in which we find ourselves."

Peter shrugged and seemed to suck something out of his teeth. The kid had down the manner of a sixty-five-year-old, the doctor noted. Peter wasn't in panic mode today. The doctor hoped he was working toward acceptance.

"I've been thinking a lot about what's immediately in front of me," Peter said. "Next year I get my driver's license. I can get a job. I can get around."

This was a positive direction. Even if Peter continued to believe he was an old man who had traveled back in time, if he could become a *happy* old man who had traveled back in time, if he could be grateful, if he could see the upside to his circumstance, he would be a long way toward becoming well adjusted. He might still be crazy, but it would be a quiet crazy that didn't interfere with his functioning in society.

"How is your band going?"

"I'm not sure that wagon is going to make it over the mountain. Daphne has invited herself into the group, and she seems to be making sparks with the middle DeVille."

Dr. Terry asked, "What's the DeVilles' family situation?"

"Three boys, single mom." Peter didn't want to let the psychiatrist know about his attraction to their mother. He steered the conversation back to safer territory.

"Lou Pitano, the music manager Barry knows, is paying for the band to record some demos."

"That's exciting, man."

"I don't know where Lou gets his money. He's probably a low-level pot dealer or something. In the music business you always start at the bottom."

"What are you hoping to work your way up to, Pete?"

"Peyote dealer, I suppose."

"Explain to me again what your job was in the delusion. When you're sixty-five."

"I work for a streaming service. For a subscription fee you can hear all kinds of music without actually buying any of it."

"A personal radio station?"

"Sort of. I'm what's called a content curator. I oversee a group of people who make playlists. 'Chill-Out Songs for After the Clubs Close,' 'Nineties Britrock,' 'Twenty Deep Tracks from Zeppelin,' or 'Sexy Soul of the Sixties.'"

"How does that work? Do people have phone lines plugged into their hi-fi systems?"

"No wires. Everyone's got a telephone in his pocket. There are little computers in every phone. You can look up anything instantly—like having an encyclopedia. People use their phones like transistor radios. You can order up a Rolling Stones song and it appears in your phone instantly."

"Do people remember the Rolling Stones?"

"The Rolling Stones are still touring."

Dr. Terry chuckled. Peter was really flying today.

"It's not just the Rolling Stones," Peter said. "What our parents and teachers think are passing teenage fads will be with us for the next half century. They just keep growing. Spider-Man and the X-Men and the Avengers are the biggest movies. The Who and Stevie Wonder. Double O fucking Seven. None of it leaves! By the time you're sixty you feel like Jacob Marley hauling these chains of teenage enthusiasm behind you as you trudge toward the grave. Maybe that's why I got pulled back here. I've been anchored by so much weight from my childhood that it finally just dragged my ass back down to the bottom of the hill."

Dr. Terry attempted a hoist. He said, "In the future, hotels on Mars?"

"The whole space-travel thing kind of petered out."

"Did they cure heart disease? Develop ESP? What's the big invention?"

"We have hundreds of TV channels. You can watch them on your phone."

"Well, tell me this, water brother—is the society you come from more equitable? Does the Woodstock generation redistribute the wealth?"

Now Peter had something to hold forth on. "When communism fell off the seesaw, capitalism shot up into the sky. No competition in the market of ideas? Well, in that case, let's raise the prices."

Dr. Terry had never seen Peter so animated. Maybe it was because he wasn't talking about himself.

"In 1970, if you put your money in a bank, the bank rewards you, right?" Peter asked. "They pay interest. In 2020, the banks charge for every service. You take money out of a bank machine? You pay a fee. You write a check? You pay a fee. And the interest is, like, one percent."

"That makes no sense, Pete. What you describe would discourage people from saving."

"The banks discourage you from saving because the banks are now also Wall Street investment services that want you to take your money out of savings and put it in stocks so they can charge you for every transaction—which they encourage you to make as often as they can scare you into it."

"Banks and stock brokerages can't be connected. It's illegal."

"Not where I come from."

"At least we didn't blow ourselves up in a nuclear war."

"Not yet. I'll tell you what I really appreciate about being in 1970: spare tires. The other day I was driving with my mother and we got a flat, and boom, there it is. Right in the trunk. A whole other tire. I put on the jack, got out the lug wrench, we were on our way in fifteen minutes. In my time, there are no spare tires. We have donuts."

The doctor asked why the two were mutually exclusive.

"Not pastries. Instead of spare tires cars come with these hard little inner tubes that you stick on until you can go to an auto shop and get your old tire fixed. But the little inner tubes can only go for sixty or seventy miles, and not over fifty miles an hour. Donuts. Worst thing about the twenty-first century. Beats COVID-19."

Dr. Terry realized he was watching a performance. Peter was riffing to avoid something.

"Speaking of donuts," Peter said, "in the twenty-first century the fast-food chains start rebranding themselves to fool the public into thinking they aren't bad for them. Dunkin' Donuts takes 'Donuts' out of their name. They're just 'Dunkin.' Kentucky Fried Chicken drops 'Fried Chicken.' They're KFC. The International House of Pancakes loses 'Pancakes'—they become IHOP. They don't make the food any better, they just change the branding."

Dr. Terry's attention was drifting. He said, "So nothing's better in the future?"

Peter closed his eyes and thought about it. He said, "The cities. We make the cities nice. Harlem is high priced. Lower Manhattan is like Beverly Hills. You can pay four million bucks for a town house in Brooklyn. If I were you, Doctor, I would pick up a couple of brownstones in Williamsburg and sit on them."

Dr. Terry said, "Peter, I think you're dreaming."

"That's what I've been trying to tell you."

The doctor checked the clock. Their time was up. They said goodbye and complimented each other on a positive session. Dr. Terry knew he had let the boy drift too far into the delusion. He had been putting on a show, and the psychiatrist wondered if it was a mistake to reward him with an audience. Progress depended not on arguing with his fantasy but in helping him to feel comfortable in the real world. If he could be steered to a place where he didn't need the delusion as a refuge, he might be weaned from it.

Nevertheless, he made a note to check on real estate prices in Brooklyn.

# TWENTY-TWO

Peter was crossing the A&P parking lot when he saw Mrs. DeVille walking toward him lugging two large grocery bags. He ran over and took them from her and carried them to her house. She let him into the kitchen. He put the bags on the counter. She offered him a root beer. He took it. No one else was home.

"Can I ask you something, Peter?" she said.

"Sure."

"How well do you know this girl Daphne?"

He took a long drink of soda while he considered his options.

"She's in my class. She's smart."

"She's fourteen, right?"

"I guess so."

"Her mother warned me to keep Rocky away from her. What she said was, 'Tell your adult son to leave my little girl alone.'"

Peter had no idea what to say. He agreed with Daphne's mother. It struck him that being Daphne's mother must be a tough job.

"I don't trust the little bitch," Mrs. DeVille said. "She smiles and uses perfect manners, but she's laughing at us behind our backs. She snaps her fingers and Rocky jumps. It's not like him at all."

There wasn't enough root beer in the world to stall as long as Peter wanted. He finally said, "She's really pretty."

"I knew girls like that," Mrs. DeVille said, in a way that let the boy know the years had not healed the old wounds. "They think they shit ice cream."

Peter laughed, and Mrs. DeVille laughed too. She said, "You got another song you can play me? Take my mind off my middle boy being seduced by that little phony?"

Peter did not protest. They went into the living room and he picked up the nylon-string guitar and played her Tom Petty's "Wildflowers." He didn't sing it very well, but he got it across.

"Where do these songs come from, Peter?" she asked. "How can you do this so well?"

Peter looked into the woman's beautiful, weathered face, and something cracked open in him. He didn't have it in him to make up any more stories.

"You know I've been under psychiatric care, right? You know I had a kind of breakdown."

She nodded.

Peter said, "My doctor asked me to write down everything I remember about the place I come from."

"East Shore Road?"

"No. The place I imagine I come from. See, Mrs. DeVille . . ." He stopped. She was regarding him with concern. He said, "Your name is Wendy, right? Would you mind if I call you Wendy?"

"That's fine."

"Terry, my psychiatrist, asked me to write down stuff I remembered about my delusion."

Peter was wearing a dungaree jacket. He fished in the pocket and pulled out the small lined notebook. He started reading:

"You think after you've had one child you know what to expect, but it's always a surprise. The twins were premature. We hadn't even started Lamaze classes yet when Janice's water broke. She was in denial; she said she had some shopping to do and would meet me at the obstetrician's office later. I demanded she get into a taxi right away. The doctor took one look at her and sent us to the hospital, where Jenny and James were born less than half an hour later. They were rushed straight into oxygen tanks in the preemie ward. Jenny was healthy enough to move into step-down in two days, but James lingered in an incubator for three weeks, intravenous tubes running into his tiny feet. He was a month old before we were able to bring him home."

Peter looked up at Mrs. DeVille. She said, "Is this a story you made up, Peter?"

"That's the million-dollar question, Wendy. All evidence says it is. But I remember it all happening. Can I read you some more?"

She said to go ahead.

"When Janice was pregnant with Peter three years later, we did everything possible in fact and theory to make sure he made it to full term. It worked. The delivery date came and went, and still he showed no sign of making an appearance. A week later Janice was waddling around the apartment sweating and swearing that if the lazy little layabout didn't hurry up and get moving, she was going to send me in after him. She did everything to speed his entrance, culminating in her insisting we take the advice of her Norwegian aunt and go out to a nightclub to drink wine and dance until labor commenced.

"If you ever want to clear a crowded punk club dance floor, step onto it with a woman so pregnant she looks like she's about to deliver a medicine ball and with a face full of determination to do it right on the spot. It worked. She went into labor and we got to the hospital, where the doctor announced that the baby was upside down with the umbilical cord wrapped around his throat. Such circumstances demanded a Cesarean delivery, but our obstetrician was old-school—he was going to reach his hand in and turn the baby around. When word of this magic trick spread through the institution, a dozen interns and medical students rushed into the delivery room to watch and learn. Janice was toughing it out with pure primal motherness when one of the students leaned into her face and said, 'You're the bass player for the Bouviers! I saw you at Maxwell's!'"

He stopped reading. He was shivering. Wendy DeVille asked him what the story meant.

"It's the most important things that happened in my life after I grew up and left Bethlehem. Wendy, I know this will convince you I'm insane, but I believe I'm a sixty-five-year-old man from the twenty-first century. I believe I woke up back in my childhood last month. I've been trying to adjust, I've been trying to get over it, I've been trying for everyone's sake to fit in and accept that it was all some kind of dream. But it doesn't feel like a dream. I don't know how to explain it, but I think it's true. And either I'm dreaming now or else something happened to me that science doesn't understand."

Wendy DeVille wore an expression that said that life's habit of handing her tough situations never stopped finding fresh innovations.

Peter forced a smile and said, "That's how nuts I am."

He handed her the notebook. She leafed through it cautiously.

"I don't know what to say to that, Peter. This is why you took your clothes off in school?"

"I was trying to shock myself awake. Didn't work."

"And you think you're sixty years old?"

"Sixty-five. I'm too old for you."

She put her hand across her mouth. "What does your doctor say?"

"Interesting case."

"What do your parents say?"

"They're walking on eggshells and hoping the doctor knows what he's doing."

"What do you want to happen?"

"I just want to be able to be honest with you, Wendy."

She got up and went into the kitchen. He stayed where he was. She came back with a plate covered with aluminum foil. She peeled it back to reveal five brownies. She put it down on the coffee table in front of him and said, "I baked these yesterday."

He said, "The songs are famous in the life I come from."

"You didn't write the songs?" It was the first time she was visibly upset by anything he had told her.

"There are two ways of looking at it," he said. "If you believe that I'm from 2020, then no, I didn't write the songs. They're all hits from the last thirty years of the twentieth century. But if you think I'm a fifteen-year-old kid who's suffering from a fantasy, then yes, I wrote them all. Which do you want me to be?"

A voice came from the kitchen. "Hello? Anybody home?"

Wendy DeVille made a cross face and called over her shoulder, "In here."

Daphne appeared. Her eyes widened when she saw the boy sitting with Mrs. DeVille.

"I was looking for Rocky. Am I interrupting?" The edges of her mouth stopped just short of a smile. The girl was a homing pigeon for mischief.

Wendy DeVille didn't give an inch. She said, "Daphne, your mother made it very clear you shouldn't be seeing Rocky, and she's right. He's eighteen years old."

"I don't believe age has anything to do with love," Daphne said happily. "Do you, Peter?"

"It really doesn't matter what you believe," Wendy told her. "Stay away from Rocky."

"Okay, Mrs. DeVille," Daphne said, switching gears, "from here on out my relationship with Rocky will be strictly professional."

Wendy shot her a what-does-that-mean glance, and Daphne smiled. "Musical. The band. We have to make our demo. Right, Peter?"

"Is Daphne in your band now, Peter?" She gave him a look that said he better not cover for this little sneak.

"I don't know if it's even a band," Peter said. "We're making a demo for Lou Pitano. Maybe that will be the end of it."

A male voice barked, "It better not be! I put my nuts on the line to get you this shot."

Barry DeVille entered from the kitchen wearing a dirty sweatshirt and acting like he hadn't disappeared the week before.

"Barry," his mother said, suddenly happy. "You must be hungry."

"Beer, Ma," Barry said. He looked at Daphne. "Why are you here?"

"I was looking for Rocky," Daphne said. She gazed at the wide-shouldered, V-shaped Barry like she might consider trading up the DeVille chain. Wendy shot her a look that could bring down a fighter jet. Daphne explained to Barry, "I'm doing some singing with the band."

"Oh you are, are ya?" Barry snickered. His mother put a brownie in his hand. He shoved it into his mouth without saying thank you. "You just decided that without me?"

"Nobody knew where you were," Peter said. As quick as it was out of his mouth, he wondered why he was defending Daphne.

"Correction," Barry said. "You didn't know where I was because I didn't care for you to know. Now let's get this straight. This is my band. I started it with my brothers, I brought in Lou P., and I'm in charge."

"Do you play an instrument, Barry?" Daphne asked sweetly. It was a jab.

Barry looked at her. "As a matter of fact, I play the drums. Maybe you heard of Joey and the Wild Ones? No? I forgot, you're a baby. I brought my brothers into my band and then I decided, after talking it over with a certain serious record producer, to step out of the lineup to manage the group. A manager needs to be objective."

Peter said, "Glad you're back, Barry. We go in with Lou to cut the demo next week."

Barry tried not to betray any surprise. He said, "That's right."

"Am I singing?" Daphne asked.

Peter started to say no and Barry cut him off. "That's undecided. I need to hear you." He looked around. "Where are Rocky and Rick?"

"They're not home," Daphne said.

Barry said, "So explain to me again—why are you two here?"

His mother offered to make Barry a sandwich, but Daphne said, "Oh, Peter and I aren't together. I just came by and interrupted him and your mom."

Mrs. DeVille fought the impulse to kick Daphne through the picture window. Barry fixed the boy with a stare a convict would give his hangman. Mrs. DeVille said, "Peter's trying to find Ricky and Rocky, too. I think they're at the go-kart track, Peter. Go look for them there. Barry, change your shirt and I'll make you some eggs. Daphne, you go home."

Peter was glad to go. Daphne had no choice. The two of them walked out the door together. In front of the house was a rusty red 1966 Dodge Charger with overhead cams and a single silver racing stripe. Barry had come home with new wheels.

They were crossing the A&P parking lot when Daphne said with delight, "Peter Wyatt, are you having an affair with my boyfriend's mother?"

She was ecstatic with the idea. It wasn't so much that she believed it as that the anticipation of telling people filled her with joy. Peter was twenty feet away from her when he heard her call out, "When you told me you had a wife, you should have told me it was someone I know!"

When he was thirty feet away she yelled, "If Rocky and I get married, you'll be my father-in-law!"

# TWENTY-THREE

Peter tried to talk to his father about his conviction that he was on a return trip from the year 2020. Howard Wyatt took a can-do, *Power of Positive Thinking* approach to the discussions. His attitude was, "It's great that we can talk this through, Pete. You have a brilliant mind, and whether at the end of this process we mutually come to the conclusion that (a) you've created an entire world in your imagination or (b) that you have indeed somehow been transported here from the future, we'll arrive at that agreement through a logical analysis of the facts. Wherever they lead."

Peter knew his father. The judge did not consider for one moment that his son had upended the laws of physics and rewound his consciousness across fifty years, but he was going to play the role of impartial judge while working to reverse-engineer the verdict he wanted to achieve.

Peter's mother gave every indication of being open to persuasion. "Let me ask you something, Peter," she said to him in the kitchen one evening when his father was in the library reviewing petitions. "Why do you define what's happened to you as your being an old man who's traveled backward in time?"

"Well, Mom," Peter said while putting away the dinner plates, "because as far as I can tell, I'm an old man who's traveled back in time."

His mother shook her head. "You misunderstand me. Let's accept that what you believe you've experienced is true. Why not define it this way: You're a fifteen-year-old boy who's somehow had a vision of his entire future life. You haven't come back, you've experienced a premonition."

Peter tossed a can of Bosco in the trash. He said, "What's the difference?"

"The difference is how you think of yourself. It seems to me that if you insist on an identity as a displaced sixty-five-year-old, as a time traveler marooned in a past century, you will never be able to adjust and move forward with your life."

"I'm not going to give up on going home to my wife and children."

"I'm not suggesting that. I'm only saying that if you accept yourself as Peter Wyatt, born in 1955, fifteen years old in 1970, and destined to live well into the next century, you can accept all this foreknowledge as a sort of gift. A gift of prophecy, if you like."

Peter leaned against the sink. He was silent, and so was his mother.

He finally said, "I appreciate what you're saying, Mom. And maybe you're right, maybe that is a positive way to think about all this. I'm not an old man who's come back but a young man who's seen the future. But my being here has already changed things. And thinking that way doesn't alter the fact that I have to return to Janice and our children."

"Don't you see, Peter?" his mother said. "You *are* returning to them. You're returning to them every day. It's just that it's going to take you a lifetime to make that journey. You shouldn't wish any of that time away."

That stopped Peter cold. What penalty would fate impose on a man who was offered a whole extra life and spurned it? What new hole was he digging for himself?

Neither of Peter's parents asked him if they would be alive in 2020, which was statistically unlikely. The father didn't ask because he believed it was all imaginary, and the mother didn't ask because she knew it would make Peter uncomfortable, and anyway, that he didn't mention them when he talked about his future life suggested the answer. She never expected to live to be ninety-eight years old.

When he found himself alone with his father, Peter tried to remember things he'd wondered about later in life and wanted to ask him. Mostly it was questions about the Wyatt family's background, which had become the subject of Thanksgiving Day speculation with his sisters after the judge had died.

Were they actually descended from the Pilgrims? Had their great-grandfather really fought at Gettysburg, and with what company? Howard was delighted that Peter was such a good audience for the family history. It was the first time any of the kids had ever cared. He even opened up about his service in the South Pacific during World War II.

They were driving home with an order of Chinese food when Peter asked him, "Dad, had you already been married before you met Mom?"

The car accelerated and the judge said, "Who told you that?"

"When I was about fifty, I got a tax bill on some property in New Hampshire I'd never heard of. I called and said it was a mistake, but the town clerk had your name and birthdate on a plot of land in the White Mountains. He said you had purchased it in 1946. I drove up there. The land was empty, just woods, but it was adjacent to a house and property that had been the home of a Mrs. Mary Appleby. I went to the town hall and checked the records. The late Mrs. Appleby had been born Mary Sotto, in Bethlehem, Rhode Island, and before she married Mr. Appleby—also deceased—she had apparently been briefly married to Howard Wyatt of Rhode Island, with whom she'd bought the house in New Hampshire. Needless to say, I was curious."

His father's face was rigid. He squeezed the steering wheel.

"Who told you about this, Peter?"

"I told you—I got a letter . . ."

"You got a letter in the future. Right. And you couldn't ask me because I was already dead? What year did all this happen?"

"A long time from now, Dad."

Howard Wyatt turned his car into the driveway of a shingled, three-story house, put it in park, and turned and faced his son.

"I need to know how you heard about this."

"Dad, I told you . . ."

"Peter—we're all with you during this tough time, but I need you to search your memory and try to remember how you really heard about this."

"It's not going to change, Dad. So, you were married to this woman . . ."

"No I was not. It was annulled. Legally, we were never married."

"It's nothing to be ashamed of."

His father stared at him. "How old are you right now?"

"You want me to say it?"

"In confidence between father and son, with God as our only witness—how old are you?"

"I'm sorry, Dad. I'm sixty-five. I heard about this around the year 2005."

"Did you tell your mother? Your sisters?"

"I didn't tell anyone. I settled the taxes and sold the lot, and that was the end of it."

Peter didn't know if the anguish in his father's face came from the hidden history coming to light or from believing his son's madness was now going to infect the family. Judge Wyatt was not a man used to making confessions. It went against his Yankee rectitude.

"Mary Sotto was a girl I knew before the war. She was a nice girl from a bad neighborhood. Her father was a drunk who would disappear on long benders, for weeks at a time. Her mother was, frankly, a tramp. When I got out of the service I saw Mary a couple of times. I guess you could say we dated. It wasn't serious. Anyway, she . . ." He could barely force out the words. "She got in trouble. She came to me. She was worried her father would beat her up, or her mother would force her to get a coat-hanger abortion. She had relatives in New Hampshire who would take her in, but only if she had a marriage certificate. The baby had to be"—he smiled coldly—"made legitimate."

"So you married her?"

"We never lived together. I went to the New Hampshire town hall with her and her aunt and her grandmother and we were married by a justice of the peace, had a nice lunch at a local restaurant that the grandmother paid for, and I kissed her on the cheek and took the train back to Rhode Island. A few months later she sent me photos of the baby, a little girl. Thirty days after that we filed for an annulment. I never saw Mary again."

Peter hesitated before asking, "Is there a chance the daughter was yours?"

His father said, "Very, very unlikely. Apparently Charlie Appleby was in the wings the whole time. He worked in the printworks, same sort as her father. A bum. Bernie Sherman knew him over there. Bernie told me later that Charlie and Mary conspired to set me up. They figured my family had money and would pay to avoid a scandal. Bernie said she never expected me to agree to marry her. I guess I was a sucker."

"The property in New Hampshire?"

"I agreed to put a down payment on a little place on the GI Bill to help set her up. Her family took over the debt after the annulment. Charlie Appleby moved right in." The judge chuckled. "Actually, he was probably there already. He was probably waiting until I got on the train to come out from behind a hedge. I didn't remember that the land behind it was a separate lot. Mary must have kept paying the taxes on it until she died." He swallowed. "And then they came looking for me and found my son. You must have thought your old man was a real phony."

"No, Dad, not at all. I just figured it was something that happened when you were young that was nobody's business. I'm glad I had a chance to ask you."

"Now you know I was a goddamn fool."

"I know what I knew already. You were a man who always did the noble thing."

A man carrying a rake appeared from behind the house and walked toward them. Howard Wyatt waved at him vaguely and backed the car into the road.

"Do you suppose this is why you came back in time, Peter?" Howard asked with a nervous smile as they drove away. "To solve the mystery of your old man's hidden wife?"

"Well," Peter told him, "if I'm gone when you wake up tomorrow, you'll know that was it."

They drove for a while before Howard said, "You were fifty when you learned about Mary Appleby?"

"More or less."

"I'm fifty this year, you know. In September."

"Fifty is a good age, Dad. You're secure and settled but still young enough to explore, to travel, to learn new things. I took up golf when I was fifty. Maybe we can play sometime."

Howard nodded, lost in thought.

When they got home with the Chinese food, his father said to Peter in a soft voice, "Don't mention any of this to your mother."

# TWENTY-FOUR

Peter told the psychiatrist he was having trouble differentiating between memories of his life in the twenty-first century and dreams.

"You know what I'm going to say to that," the doctor replied.

"Yeah, I know—my life in the twenty-first century *was* a dream," Peter said. "I appreciate that it's hard for you to accept being a figment of my imagination."

"It's sort of demeaning," the doctor said, and then scratched his nose.

"Last night I was thinking back on my last day in 2020. I was floating on my back in a pool looking up through the leaves at a blue sky. My ears were underwater and I could hear the humming of the pumps and filters. There was music, too. The Beatles' *Let It Be* album. 'Across the Universe.'"

"More details. Tell me about your pool."

"It's a stone pool in a meadow surrounded by trees, with outdoor speakers attached to an old barn we converted into a pool house."

The doctor said it sounded great.

Peter said, "I'm sure that was where I was when I left. When I came here. I think I fell asleep in the pool listening to the Beatles and woke up in my childhood bedroom in 1970."

"Good thing you weren't listening to Beethoven—you might have come to in the Napoleonic Wars."

Peter continued: "I keep returning to the idea that I drowned in the pool. Maybe lost consciousness and inhaled a lot of water before they found me. Brain damage. I might be in the hospital now while my wife argues with the doctors. I'd like to get a signal to her that I'm conscious in here."

The psychiatrist knew there was a proper way to respond to a formulation like that, but he followed his gut. He said, "Why don't you try wiggling your toes, blinking your eyes. Tap out SOS with your forefinger."

Peter blinked rapidly and drummed his fingers. He could have been wiggling his toes at the same time.

This went on for a while. The doctor said, "We have to hope they got the signal. I want to try something else. Let's go out to my car."

"Where are we going?"

"Not leaving the driveway. In my Corvette I have an eight-track player, and among my tapes is *Let It Be*."

"If you had a swimming pool, we could get really scientific."

"Peter, this is about as scientific as a séance."

Peter and the doctor went out the door of the white house and climbed into a Corvette convertible with the top down. The doctor yanked a Santana tape out of the changer and fished around behind the seat for the Beatles eight-track. He inserted it. The music surrounded them. "Two of Us." "Dig a Pony." Peter closed his eyes and tipped the passenger's seat back as far as it would go. The doctor sat with his hands on the steering wheel, staring through the windshield at the flagpole in the front yard of the house across the street. Beneath the Stars and Stripes flew a POW/MIA banner. The doctor and the boy sat in silence while the music played. When the first track began again, the boy said, "Keep it going."

The doctor said they were already over fifty minutes. Peter said, "I'm your last patient of the day, right? And we're sitting in your car listening to the Beatles. Come on."

The doctor said okay. He thought they might get somewhere. "I've Got a Feeling." "One After 909."

"You once told me you were thinking about your Christmas shopping when you left the future."

"It was the middle of December; I was almost out of time."

"But your last memory of 2020 is floating in your swimming pool, looking up at the sky through the branches of an apple tree."

Peter looked like he had something to defend. The doctor pressed on.

"Do trees bloom and people swim outside in December where you come from?"

Peter thought about it. "I must have that wrong. Maybe I was remembering something about Christmas shopping while I was in the pool. I'm old, my mind wanders. Memories get crossed."

"So it was summer when you departed."

"Must have been."

"Summer of 2020."

"Had to be."

Peter folded his hands and moved his legs together and leaned forward.

"This world, this post–World War II society you live in, Terry. It goes away. I don't come from a place where everybody's parents came through the Depression and World War II, where the adults tried to give the kids everything they never had, where the kids rebelled against materialism. This world of the New Deal and the Great Society and the Atlantic Alliance is gone. It slipped away without us even noticing. It's as dead as the lost airmen of the Pacific campaign. It's as dead as the flower children."

"Kid, I'm sitting right beside you."

"Why did I come back here?"

"We're working on that."

"Why did I come back to live among ghosts?"

The doctor looked directly into the boy's eyes. "There's more of them than there are of us."

"More of who?"

"The dead."

"How old are you, Doctor? What year were you born?"

"Nineteen thirty-seven."

"You might be alive, still, in 2020."

"I do hope to stick around till they legalize pot like you promised."

"My friends are getting old. They tell you that if you live through your sixties, odds are you'll live into your eighties, and everybody says that's great news. Then you find out how tough it is to live through your sixties! Monica has heart disease. Annie had a brain aneurysm. Steve has a tumor on his bladder. Mark had a stroke. Mike has throat cancer. Jim got diagnosed with Parkinson's. And prostate cancer—half the guys I play poker with are watchfully waiting. We compare PSA numbers like golf scores."

The doctor said, "What's your prognosis?"

"Me? I've been lucky so far."

"No issues? Exercise?"

"Yeah, I go to the gym. I swim."

"Close your eyes. Tell me again about your swimming pool. You said there was a humming?"

"The pool filters. It's a steady hum. You don't even notice it until your ears are under water."

"And the apple tree over your head, looking up."

"Yes. I was looking through the branches at the blue sky."

"Kind of strange."

"What is?"

"An apple tree with branches hanging over a pool. Don't apples drop into the water? Mess up the pool, muck up the filters, draw flies? Why do you have an apple tree branching over your pool?"

Peter considered. "They must fall on the grass."

"But you told me over and over, you were looking straight up through the branches."

"Yes. I was. But there were no apples."

"You said there were apples on the branch."

"There were." Peter was confused.

The doctor said, "Tell me again about your friends and their illnesses."

"Well. Everybody had something. In 2020, it's not like here. Here, they find cancer and you're dead in a year. Where I come from, they detect it really early and they have all kinds of treatments. Immunotherapy. The CyberKnife. Some guys I know let the surgeon plant radioactive pellets in their prostates! I said, 'I don't want radioactive anything inside me! Take it all out! Get the fucking disease out of me!'"

The doctor looked at Peter steadily. He wasn't playing the smiling hippie. He said, "So you did have it."

Peter's body unfolded. He was puzzled. He said, "I didn't. . . . What a thing to . . ."

The doctor said nothing. They listened to the Beatles. "Get Back."

Peter said, "Something happened. I went in for my annual checkup. I had skipped a year. When we went to Spain I missed my physical. The doctor stuck his finger up my ass, and instead of making his usual bad joke he left the room. I waited for him to come back. I put my clothes on. I thought he had to check on another patient. Instead, the nurse came in and handed me a card and said, 'Go see this doctor, he's a specialist.' I said, 'A specialist in what?' She said, 'Urinary.' She didn't look me in the eye. When I went down the corridor, my doctor had closed the door to his office."

"You must have been scared."

"I was confused. It seemed like they were being mysterious, but I didn't think I could have anything seriously wrong with me. I felt fine. I went to the specialist, and he stuck a rod up my ass without warning me. That hurt. Then he told me, 'Okay, you can go now.' I said, 'You haven't told me what you're looking for.' He said, 'Oh, you have an enlarged prostate.' I was almost laughing when I left the building. I figured I was off the hook. Every man my age has an enlarged prostate. That's why the restroom lines are so long at a Willie Nelson concert.

"I put it out of my mind. Then out of the blue, I'm driving to work on a Monday morning, coming down from the country, and my phone rings. I hit the button and it's the ass doctor. He says, 'I got the results of the biopsy, and unfortunately there's some cancer.' That was all I heard. He was talking about a very limited radius and lucky we caught it early—but what I heard was I had cancer. It seemed impossible. It was like he'd told me I was Nigerian. There was a population I had always been in, and now I was being moved to a different population on the other side of the world."

Dr. Terry said, "You don't have cancer now. In 1970."

Peter was astonished at his own memories. He said, "No. I don't have cancer in 1970. I'm just a kid."

"Where was the apple tree again?"

"The apple tree branch hangs over our pool . . ."

"Yeah? And the humming?"

"The filters."

"And the music?"

"The outdoor speakers."

"Tell me again what the music was."

"The Beatles' *Let It Be* album. It took me back to being fifteen, when there was endless empty time."

"It took you back. You were stressed about the cancer so you floated in your pool, listening to the Beatles."

The eight-track clicked. "Across the Universe."

Peter said, "No."

"No?"

"It was almost Christmas. I was looking up at the apple tree and pretending I was in the pool."

"Where were you?"

"I was in a LINAC. Every day. Every morning for ten weeks."

"What's a LINAC?"

"A linear particle accelerator. It's a big tube they slide you inside to shoot radiation into you."

The doctor let the boy take his time.

"I had surgery, and they didn't get it all. I was in my second round of radiation. The first one didn't do anything. The oncologist said, 'Going in again is a long shot, but hey, what do you have to lose?'"

Dr. Terry looked at a fifteen-year-old face wearing the exhaustion of an old man.

"I was in a radiation tube. Every day. I took the subway up there in the morning and drank seven cups of water, and they called me in and loaded me into the big radiology machine like a bullet going into the chamber of a pistol. The prostatectomy didn't get it all. That was a sad day, when we got that news. I did one long round of radiation in the spring, but the PSA kept climbing. We tried a second round, along with hormone shots to slow it down. I would lie on that tray and they would slide me into the tube up to my chest, and I would stare at the ceiling where they had painted an apple tree against a summer sky. And they would play the Beatles over the speakers to drown out the hum of the radiation machine, and I thought, 'Doesn't that tree with the apples look like the tree that hangs over our pool? Six months and I'll be back there.' Five days a week for ten weeks. And in the end it didn't stop the cancer."

The doctor waited to see if the boy would say anything else. He did not.

"So you came here."

"I guess so."

"Now we know."

"We don't know how to get me back."

"Peter." Terry Canyon put his hand on Peter's arm. "There's nothing there for you to go back to."

Peter's eyes turned red and he said, "I should have seen it right away. Why else would I be sent to live among ghosts? I must be a ghost too."

# TWENTY-FIVE

Well, I went back to see about it once
Went back to straighten it out
Everybody that I talked to had seen us there
Said they didn't know who I was talking about

—Bob Dylan, "Red River Shore"

Most days Peter's mother woke before dawn. She would lie on her back in the half light and listen to the old house breathe. She knew the whispers and cracks, the hiss of the pipes in the walls in the winter. Now, in the spring, birds were singing scales through the window screens. Squirrels leaped from the roof to high branches. She hung suspended between waking and dreaming, her awareness flowing through the pulsing life in the green around them. She imagined she could feel in her own chest the rapid breathing of the rabbits crouched under the hedges, the crows perched on thin limbs, the moles nosing through the woods. This dream space between unconsciousness and waking was the only time that was completely hers.

Howard loved the farm, but in her heart she wished they had never left the ranch house where the children were born. It was crowded but filled with life. She liked having neighbors on all sides, she liked being immersed in community. What they had now was the dream Howard had worked for. It was never her dream. She never told him. The girls were grown and gone now. Only Peter, the baby, was at home. It was too many rooms for them already.

Since Peter's problems appeared, she no longer allowed herself to drift back to sleep at daybreak. When she first woke now, she was up for the day. She recognized a creaking in the floorboards in the corridor. Peter was walking. She knew all her children's footfalls. When the girls were little she and Howard would be in the living room watching TV and there would be a groan in the ceiling and she would say, "Cathy's up." Howard would ask how she knew it was Cathy and not Sally or Peter or the sound of the house settling, and she would go upstairs and find Cathy making her way to the bathroom half-asleep. Fathers didn't even know how little they knew.

She went into the hall and found Peter in sneakers, gym shorts, and a sweatshirt. It was 5:00 a.m. She asked where he was going.

"For a run, Mom. This body is so resilient. I can run for miles, sit down for five minutes, and run again. No soreness in my knees, no stiffness afterward. My heart is indestructible. And my senses—they're all turned up. The scent of hyacinths in our yard is like candy. Yesterday I grabbed a tomato from Mr. North's garden. It was like biting into Eden. Every cell in me is alert. I wonder if you'd drive me to the public pool when I come back? I'd love to do some laps before school."

She was concerned. He looked at her with sympathy.

"I'm not manic, Mom," he said. "I'm trying to see my being here as a blessing. I'm going to learn to accept it as a gift. I have so much energy, stamina. I want to take advantage of it while I can."

The last three words bothered her. She said, "Go run. I'll start breakfast."

He kissed her cheek and said, "Oatmeal, okay? Or fruit. No bacon, no white bread. I love you, Mom."

She put on her robe and went downstairs to the kitchen. When he returned, pink-faced and shining with sweat, he ate oatmeal and strawberries. She served him and then sat with him and engaged with the delusion.

"Do you feel any more settled now, Peter? In this time?" she asked.

He wasn't going to tell her about the cancer. There was no reason for her to know.

He said, "I know how nuts it sounds, Mom, but I still have all the memories of a sixty-five-year-old man from 2020. I know it's scary for you to hear me say that, and I appreciate being able to discuss it rationally." She nodded, and he took a bite of strawberry and added, "I also appreciate that *rationally* is an odd word to use in this circumstance."

"How do you imagine you got here?"

"I'm willing to accept any explanation. Religion, science fiction, sorcery. I would subscribe to any narrative that eventually returned me to my wife and kids."

His mother asked him to tell her about them.

"A girl and two boys. They're pretty much grown. The youngest is in college now. University of California."

"California? Didn't you tell us you lived in New York?"

"In the future kids from all over the country compete for the same colleges. It's not like now when you go to the best school you can get into within sixty miles of home. When I went to Dartmouth, my friends were astonished I was going out of state."

His mother looked surprised. She said, "You got into Dartmouth?"

"SATs, Mom. Turns out I test well. All your worry is for nothing."

"Tell me about your wife."

"You would love Janice. You will love her. She's smart, she's funny. She's a fierce mother. Comes from Long Beach, Long Island. Her father was chief of police! Gus Crowley. Tough guy, but really decent. Almost made a Mets fan out of me."

"And your children?"

"Your grandchildren, Mom. James is a sportsman. From the time he was little he was always going fishing, riding bikes and skateboards. He played lacrosse in college. He works for a company selling athletic equipment now, just to pay the rent. Jenny is like you—a scholar. Speaks four languages. Did a summer internship at NATO in Belgium. She's teaching in DC now, hoping to get into the diplomatic corps. Pete Junior is doing film studies. He makes money working as an extra in every movie and TV show shot in LA. Janice and I go to the movies and look for him. He saves his money, and when classes are out he heads off to Mexico or Europe or Alaska. Last summer he backpacked across China!"

Peter's voice got softer. He said, "I understand that the evidence is that none of this is real. That Janice and our family don't exist. That the world isn't turning out to be how I remember it. I understand I may have come to the end of that life and been given the gift of starting again. But for all that, I do believe I'll find a way back to them."

His mother took his empty oatmeal bowl and his plate and put them in the sink and turned on the faucet.

She spoke to him without turning around. She said, "Every life has layers, Peter. Everyone has things they don't talk about. It doesn't make them less real. It might make them more precious. I don't understand why you're going through this challenge right now. But I know it will be easier for you if you find a way to behave so that the world won't throw barriers up at you."

"Pretend I'm not crazy, you mean."

"You're not crazy. Maybe you really are foreseeing your future life, picking up signals in some way we don't understand. It may become a source of strength for you. It could become an advantage. But only if you behave discreetly. If you talk about this to people who don't love you, it will hurt you." She turned off the water and looked him in the eye. "Do you agree with me?"

"Blend in."

"Try."

He pushed his chair back from the table and stood. She thought he had grown another inch in the last week. He was already taller than his father.

He said, "It's good advice, Mom. Thank you."

His mother told him to get dressed and she would drop him at the pool. On the drive over she told him a story.

"You know I was raised Catholic, Peter. I drifted away from it in college, and your father's family was somewhat prejudiced, so we married in the Episcopal church. But when I was a little girl I was very concerned with exactly how it all worked. The logic behind the Scriptures and teachings. In catechism class the nun told us that there was no conception of time in heaven. Once you ascended to paradise, you could look back at all of human history like a picture book. You could skip from the dinosaurs to the cowboys, back to the creation and forward to the end of time. I raised my hand and asked if that meant that when we got to heaven we could look back at our own lives on Earth. The sister said, 'Yes, you surely could.' I said, 'You mean I might be in heaven right now, looking at myself asking you this question?' The sister said, 'Well, yes. But we don't know for sure if you are going to heaven.' I said, 'And we can pray to the saints in heaven for intercession with the Lord? To hear our petitions?' The sister agreed that was true. I said, 'Well, then, assuming I will someday get to heaven, that means I can pray to myself for help right now!' I was sent home from Sunday school with a note from the Mother Superior saying I needed to stop being such a smarty-pants.

"My mother was a rigorous thinker, a Catholic intellectual. She raced right over to the convent and defended me. I never did hear exactly what she said to the nuns, but I was treated with respect in Sunday school from that day forward."

"Strong mothers," Peter said. "An inherited attribute."

"That's not the story I want to tell you. It's what my mother said to me about time. After she came back from seeing the sisters, my mother said that time is like a winding river. If you're sitting on the bank of the river and a motorboat goes by in the morning, by noon that boat is in your past. And if there's a sailboat coming slowly toward you, still a mile away, that sailboat is in your future. That's the nature of time. But imagine a man standing on top of a mountain looking down at the river. To him, you, the motorboat, and the sailboat are all visible at once. He can see what to you is past, present, and future. Time isn't fixed. Time depends on where you're watching from."

Peter considered the story. He never remembered his mother talking to him like this. They pulled up to the public swimming pool.

She said, "The universe is mysterious, Peter. I can't guess why you're here, but don't be in a hurry to leave us. As long as you're here, try to live fully in the time you're given."

Peter swam for an hour, showered, and walked to school. First period was English. He was standing in the corridor outside the classroom, thinking about his mother's advice, when he saw his old crush Amy Blessen coming toward him, carrying her books. Her hair as blond as sun, her eyes as blue as sea, her skin as brown as sand. He took a deep breath, like a diver.

He said, "Amy, I saw the end of the field hockey game. You were great."

If she was surprised to have the crazy boy speak to her, she didn't show it. She said, "Thanks, Peter. It was a good game."

"Hey, I was thinking. I have tickets for James Taylor at Brown on Saturday. Would you like to go?"

Peter thought time was stopping all over again. Amy looked surprised, and then she smiled. "Sure, I'd like to see James Taylor."

"Great," Peter said. "It's part of their spring weekend. He plays outside Saturday afternoon."

"Oh, in the afternoon? Saturday afternoons we have games."

"Ah, okay. Well, just an idea."

"I wish I could."

The bell rang, and they both went into class. Peter didn't feel sixty-five. He didn't feel fifteen either. He felt neither old nor young. He felt like he was standing on top of a mountain, looking down at the boats in a winding river.

# TWENTY-SIX

Peter gave the DeVilles a cassette with some more songs he thought they could do at their demo session, "Radar Love" and "Taking Care of Business" among them. Rocky asked him to write something for Daphne to sing, and the boy gave them a tape of himself singing a falsetto version of "Afternoon Delight." It was meant to discourage Daphne's joining in on the recording, but she said she loved it and made the DeVilles learn to play it. Lou Pitano said it was the best song of the bunch.

So it was a surprise when Peter went to a band meeting at the DeVille house and they fired him.

"We intend to keep you on as a writer," Lou Pitano explained. "But we're going with Daphne as the singer. Frankly, Peter, I have a certain image in mind, and you don't fit it. Nothing personal. Ricky, Rocky, and Barry have a look."

"Well," Peter pointed out, "they are brothers."

"Exactly," Lou said. "And Daphne, she's this beautiful flower child."

"I get the picture," Peter said. He was offended in principle but not particularly disappointed. His goal was to make some money on music publishing, not become Foghat.

Lou Pitano would certainly be upset when he found out that Peter had copyrighted all the songs and they wouldn't be able to release them without his permission, but he decided to sit on that information for a while.

Barry DeVille was strutting around the room like a bouncer, waiting for any excuse to toss Peter out on his ass. Daphne was folded into Rocky like he was her chair. Their fingers were entwined.

The only thing that hurt Peter's feelings was that his new friend Ricky had gone along with the coup. Peter looked at Ricky, his long hair covering his aviator glasses, and said, "You agree with this, Rick?"

Ricky DeVille looked up with intensity and snapped, "Never get between family."

Peter didn't know what that meant. Barry stopped pacing and glared at him. Then Peter got it. He looked at Daphne, who affected a false concern. She had surely suggested to the brothers that Peter had eyes for their mother. Under those circumstances he was lucky he hadn't ended up strung from a ceiling fan like Mrs. Quigly's cat.

Wendy DeVille was nowhere to be seen. Her sons had picked a time when she wouldn't be home to excommunicate the interloper.

Peter stood and shrugged and asked if they wanted him at the recording session anyway. They were doing his songs . . .

Barry said no. Lou Pitano got up and, taking the boy by the elbow, walked him to the door. He stepped outside with him and whispered, "Nobody likes a smartass."

Waiting on the street was Daphne's friend Pasa. Peter assumed she had been sent outside while the ax fell, but it was quickly apparent that she had no idea what was going on with the DeVille brothers' band.

"Peter," she said in a whisper. "Is Daphne in there?"

"Uh, yeah, Pasa. Why don't you go knock?"

She jumped back. "Oh no. I'm not going into that house. Daphne's mother called my house looking for her. She told her mom we were having a sleepover. Now my mom's freaking out and Daphne's mother is threatening to call the police and have Rocky arrested for contributing to the delinquency of a minor. Would you please go back and warn her to maybe get out of there before the cops come?"

Peter stood there thinking about it.

"You know, Pasa," he said, "the greatest act of friendship we could show Daphne might be for us to do nothing and let the law take its course. Get her away from that Manson family before she's hopelessly corrupted."

Pasa nodded.

Peter figured that if Rocky ended up in jail for statutory rape, they would have to let him back in the band. It was cruel, but he was more hurt than he was ready to let on.

# TWENTY-SEVEN

They ate dinner early in 1970. By five thirty the dishes were cleared and the TV went on. The local news, then Walter Cronkite, then some black-and-white rerun before prime time started at seven thirty. *The Courtship of Eddie's Father*, *Room 222*, *The Johnny Cash Show*. No one paid attention to what was on; the TV screen was like a fireplace. Peter's mother read a Gore Vidal paperback while his father looked through the *Saturday Review*. Both parents had cigarettes lit and resting on ashtrays. Peter's homework was spread out on the carpet. He was trying to think of something to say about *Ethan Frome*.

The sports report was on in the background. Peter heard the words "Long Beach, Long Island." His wife's hometown. He looked up at the screen.

"Many hockey fans called him the greatest goalie of all time. Sawchuk achieved fame with the Detroit Red Wings and was a New York Ranger when his famous temper got him into the barroom brawl that killed him. Terry Sawchuk, dead at forty."

The sports reader went on to talk about the Red Sox. Peter

was alert now. He said, “Dad—who is Sawchuk? Hockey player who just died?”

His father looked over his reading glasses. “Terry Sawchuk? Used to play with the Bruins.”

“They said his home was in Long Beach, Long Island.”

His parents stared at him.

Peter spoke awkwardly. “Long Beach, Long Island, is where my wife comes from. Came from.”

His father looked pained.

Peter said, “She grew up on Sawchuk Road.”

His mind was carouseling. After he heard the new Beatles song, after Rockefeller died, he had phoned Long Island information looking for the Crowleys on Sawchuk Road in Long Beach and was told by the operator there was no such listing and no such street. That was when he began to accept that the life he remembered was a delusion. What if Sawchuk Road had a different name in 1970? Hope and panic rose in him.

His parents looked worried.

He said, “In my dream, my delusion, I married a woman named Janice Crowley from Sawchuk Road in Long Beach, Long Island. I’ve been to her family’s house a hundred times. If we could drive down there . . .”

His father said, “Peter, we are not going to drive a hundred and fifty miles looking for—what?”

“Proof,” Peter said.

His mother said, “Peter, it wouldn’t change anything.”

“It’s my wife, Mom! If my wife is alive in this . . . reality, I have to know it! And if she exists, if there is a Janice Crowley in Long Beach and her father, Gus, is a cop and her mom, Virginia, works at the local junior college and her brother, Tim, is studying to become an ophthalmologist—if all that turns out to be true, doesn't it prove that I really have traveled here from later?"

Howard said, "You know that the world isn't how you expected it to be. It's not how you remembered it. Let's be patient, Pete. Give me the information and I'll make some calls."

Peter said, "If it turns out my wife is alive . . ."

"It wouldn't put you back in the twenty-first century," his mother said. "They wouldn't even know you."

Peter said hopefully, "Unless Janice came back too."

"She'd have found you. We're easy to find."

"Her dad was an undercover detective in 1970." Peter's voice was rising. "Of course they had an unlisted number."

"You're reaching, Pete," his father said.

Peter regretted upsetting them. They could do nothing to help, and he was a fool to reveal his thoughts.

His mother said, "Remember what we talked about, Peter. Don't call attention."

Peter stopped talking about it. He finished his homework and went to his room. He set up the small portable electric typewriter his sister Cathy had left behind when she got married. He carefully typed out transfers of copyright on "Racing in the Street" and "Wildflowers" to Wendy DeVille of 486 Buttongreen Lane, Bethlehem, Rhode Island. He got a second sheet of paper and signed over "Smokin' in the Boys' Room" and "School's Out" to Barry, Ronald, and Richard DeVille. Then he typed up a third page giving title to the original composition "Afternoon Delight" to Daphne Burrows. He found three envelopes and addressed them.

At breakfast he asked his father to witness the documents

and stamp them with his notary seal. His father figured it was no stranger than most of what his son did lately.

Peter stopped at a mailbox across from the school and dropped in the envelopes.

He went to his morning classes. He didn't raise his hand. He did nothing to call attention to himself. In the hallway outside the cafeteria he stopped his friend John North, who was carrying the newly arrived West Bethlehem Veterans Memorial High School yearbook.

"John," he said, "I know I've been acting weird lately. This is going to seem strange too. I want to write something in your yearbook."

John North handed over the book. Peter flipped to the faculty section and wrote over the photo of Mr. Mosspaw: "Microsoft. Apple. Amazon. Google." He handed the yearbook back to John North and said, "Remember those names. In the years to come, if you see new companies with those names starting up, buy stock. Tell Mr. Mosspaw too. I wouldn't steer you wrong."

Peter ate lunch alone. He ate something that was supposed to be macaroni. He saw Delores with the smile buttons on a stepladder hanging posters for the prom. Mina Habib was yelling up at her, demanding that all proms be canceled in honor of the Kent State victims.

When the bell rang, Peter took back his tray and walked out of the high school. He headed directly to the DeVilles' house. He knocked on the kitchen door. No one was home. He expected that. Wendy would be at work. The boys could be anywhere. Barry's '66 Charger was in the driveway. He was likely wandering the neighborhood, selling drugs or fireworks or otherwise unknitting the social fabric. Peter opened the car door and looked on top of the visor and reached under the seat. He found the keys in the ashtray. Barry was too much of a badass to not leave his keys in the car. Who would fuck with the toughest hood in town? Nobody who ever intended to come back.

Peter turned over the engine. It made more noise than it needed to. A stick shift; it had been a while. There was an eight-track pushed into the dashboard. Hendrix. "Voodoo Child (Slight Return)." Getaway music.

Peter backed out of the driveway and steered toward the interstate. He had no license. He was driving a stolen car. He was fifteen years old. He was going to New York to find his wife.

# TWENTY-EIGHT

Terry Canyon rolled up the Wyatts' driveway on his Triumph to find Peter's mother coming out of the house to meet him. She was distraught.

"Mr. Mosspaw called to say that Peter disappeared from school!"

Terry turned off his engine and dropped the kickstand. He said, "He might be cutting class. He's a kid."

Joanne Wyatt showed him a note in the boy's handwriting. *I love you, Mom, but I have to go home now. Don't feel bad. —P.*

"Have you checked with his friends?"

"I called the DeVilles' house. Mrs. DeVille said her son's car was stolen this afternoon right out of their driveway."

"You think Peter stole a car? Can he drive?"

"I didn't know it, but if he thinks he's sixty-five . . ."

"Where would he go?"

"He got upset at something on the news last night. He decided that he knew where his wife was living and wanted me to drive him to, to somewhere on Long Island, I think. I can't remember where."

Dr. Terry was thinking in psychiatrist triple speed. Like a tennis pro, he was processing the information flying at him to formulate a useful response. He became aware of a loud engine getting closer. A silver MG sports car was coming up the driveway fast.

"It's him!" the mother shouted and ran toward the car. The MG stopped and Wendy DeVille climbed out. She was dressed in the short blue zipper uniform of a dental assistant and matching eye shadow. Neither the mother nor the doctor had any idea who she was.

Wendy said, "Mrs. Wyatt?"

The mother thought this new person was a nurse come to tell her horrible news.

"I'm Wendy DeVille. Ricky's mother."

Relieved and surprised, Joanne Wyatt asked, "Do you know where Peter is?"

"I have this." Wendy held out a pocket-size notebook.

"That's the journal I gave Peter," Terry Canyon said.

Wendy handed it to him. She said, "Are you Peter's father?"

"No, I'm Terry Canyon, I'm his . . . I'm a friend of the family."

"Terry Canyon. You're the psychiatrist."

"May I see that?" Joanne Wyatt reached for the journal.

Wendy said, "Peter writes about his wife's family's house in Long Beach, New York. He goes into a lot of detail. I think that might be where he's gone."

Peter's mother could make no sense of this. Why did this woman know Peter's secret? How did she get his private journal, and what was she doing reading it? She wished her husband were home. She had left urgent messages at the courthouse and been told the judge was in the middle of an important trial. No doubt it was, she thought. And no doubt it would fall to the mother to save their boy.

# TWENTY-NINE

Barry DeVille's 1966 Dodge Charger had four bucket seats—three brown, one yellow—a 318-cubic-inch V8 engine, a three-speed floor shifter, and an AM radio. A piece of the floorboard was gone on the passenger's side. Peter could look over and see the road speeding by through the hole. The car wasn't old enough to be so thoroughly rusted. The previous owner must have parked it by the ocean all year and never washed off the salt.

The fuel gauge was under half a tank. Peter had little cash. It comforted him to see 59 CENTS A GALLON posted on the gas stations that he passed. Just over the Connecticut line he went by a speed trap doing seventy-five. The trooper didn't move. In 1970 you had to hit eighty to get a ticket on Route 95.

The turnpike was a series of tollbooths and Howard Johnsons. Someday the tolls would be taken out, after too many semis jackknifed on approach. Someday McDonald's would win the highway concession away from HoJo's, too. None of that had happened yet. The Hendrix tape was going around for the second time when Peter yanked it out and the radio came on.

The announcer had big news. Hot off the peace treaty in Vietnam, Henry Kissinger had announced a surprise deal with Red China to recognize Taiwan as an independent nation. Both Chinas would be admitted to the United Nations. It was another foreign policy triumph for the Nixon administration.

"No no no!" Peter whacked the steering wheel. "That doesn't happen!"

He pressed the gas and began to recite memories of his life with Janice. Janice at their wedding reception dancing with her father, Janice on their honeymoon catching a tuna in the Caribbean, Janice riding a bike on Nantucket with Pete Junior in a baby seat. He would not let her go. He would find his way back to her.

The news said to stand by for Kissinger. Peter punched the button to change the station. A preacher was reading from Psalm 126: "When the Lord brought back the captives of Zion, we were like men dreaming. Then was our mouth filled with laughter, and our tongue with rejoicing."

He hit the button again. A buzzing John Lee Hooker riff came out of the static. "When I die, he's gonna set me up with the spirit in the sky." Peter decided the radio was talking to him. He drove under a highway bridge and the music faded until he came out the other side.

He went around a turn coming toward the Mystic exit and a bang rattled the whole automobile, followed by a gruesome scraping sound. Peter looked in the mirror and saw a trail of sparks behind him. He pulled over onto the shoulder and got out, other cars shooting past. A burned black scar on the tar tracked his path. He got down on the ground and peered under the Charger. The rear bolts holding the tailpipe had let go and the pipe was dragging. He got on his back and pushed himself under the car. The undercarriage was rusted through. Even if he'd had bolts and tools, there was nothing to attach the tailpipe to. Barry DeVille's new acquisition was never going to pass inspection, no matter how much he bribed the mechanic. The boy wiggled out from under the car and opened the trunk. The foot of a jack and no crowbar, a spare tire covered in patches, a spent tube of Super Glue. He sat down by the side of the road and tried to imagine what story he could tell the highway cop who would surely be there within ten minutes unless he figured out a way to get back on the road.

He had a wide brown belt with a thick buckle around his thin waist. He pulled it off and slid back under the car. He wrapped his belt around the south end of the tailpipe, binding it to the driveshaft. He knew that as soon as the tailpipe heated up it would begin sawing through the leather—but if it held for ninety minutes it would get him to his wife's house. After that, nothing mattered.

Thirty miles behind him, his mother's station wagon was pulling onto the highway. Dr. Terry Canyon sat in the passenger's seat reading a Texaco map, while behind him Wendy DeVille recited details about the boy's wife's family's house from his pocket journal.

"He says it's a three-story house with a detached garage off Beech Street, two blocks from the ocean. It's got a red roof, but that might be in the future."

Peter's mother gripped the steering wheel with both hands and pushed the accelerator down with her foot.

Terry Canyon said, "Long Beach looks pretty small. It's an island. If we can get to New London in forty-five minutes, we can make the next ferry. That will be quicker than going all the way down to the Whitestone Bridge."

Joanne Wyatt hit eighty. Dr. Terry said be careful you don't get a ticket. She said her husband was a judge.

Dr. Terry turned and looked at Wendy. He said, "Your son flipping out about Peter taking his car?"

Wendy shook her head. "It doesn't take much for Barry to flip out. He's been in and out—" She stopped herself. "He's had a hard time. His daddy left home when he was small, and he tried to be the man of the house. He didn't have very good examples."

"I can talk to him if you want me to," Dr. Terry said.

Wendy looked at him for a moment. She said, "You mean professionally?"

"Not officially, no," Terry said. "Does he like motorcycles?"

"He likes anything fast and loud that he can hurt himself on."

"Well, there ya go. Common ground. You have three boys, right?"

"I do."

"Well, maybe one weekend when Pete's back and Barry's car is recovered we all go up to Laconia and watch the motorcycle races. Pitch a tent, cook some hot dogs, talk about the world."

Wendy was uncertain if this was a generous offer from a professional therapist or a pickup line from a good-looking charmer. Peter's mother was itching to slam on the brakes and send them both through the windshield, but she forced herself to concentrate on the mission at hand.

# THIRTY

The fat orange sun was sinking in a gasoline sky when the stolen Charger lurched over the bridge into the hometown of Peter's wife. He could smell the ocean. Long Beach wasn't as developed as the picture in his mind, but neither was it suburban. The shingled single-family houses were pushed close together with small yards separated by chain-link barriers and an occasional beat-up picket fence.

He got turned around looking for landmarks. He was almost clipped by a garbage truck coming down the wrong side of a street that had been one-way in his memory. He pulled over and climbed onto the hood of the car and looked up and down and across the yards and spotted the steeple of a church on the block where his wife grew up. In four minutes he had found her house. He parked across the street and turned off the engine.

On the small front lawn of her father's house, Janice Crowley, age ten, was turning cartwheels.

"She exists," Peter said out loud. The little girl on the lawn was familiar to him from black-and-white photos in his wife's family album, from scratchy home movies played on Christmas Day. He was amazed that she was in full color and three dimensions. In every step she took, in every shake of her head, in every wrinkle of her nose, it was Janice. She had come back to him.

He sat watching her for a long time. He didn't know what to do next. She ran into the house, and he despaired. Four minutes later she came out again, carrying a green hula-hoop. The streetlights came on. Soon she would disappear back inside. He got out of the car and walked to the edge of the yard.

"Hey," he said.

She looked up at him. She was neither curious nor interested. She said hello and went back to her hula-hoop.

"You're pretty good at that," he said.

She counted spins: "Eleven, twelve, thirteen . . ."

"You're Janice."

She stopped spinning and looked at him.

"Are Tim and your folks inside?"

She said, "You know my brother?"

"Sort of." He took a step onto the lawn. He was working without a net now. "Do you know me? I'm Peter."

"I don't know."

"What grade are you in, Janice?"

"Grade four."

A door slammed open and a familiar New York accent demanded, "Hey! Who the hell are you?"

The boy looked around and broke into a grin. "Gus!"

The compact man was moving toward him, out of the house and across the lawn. "Who are you?"

"I'm Peter. Peter Wyatt. You look good, Gus! You look so young!"

In 1970 Gus Crowley was an undercover narcotics officer working around the New York beaches and airports. It was a dangerous job. He wore a walrus mustache and shaggy hair to blend in with the criminals he pursued. He lived with the fear that one of them would learn where he lived and threaten his family. He was always on alert. One look at this kid's eyes pushed all his panic buttons.

Gus got close to the boy's face and said, "Tell me who you are and what you want."

Peter couldn't stop grinning. His wife was real. His remembered life was not a delusion. He looked at his father-in-law and said, "I know this is going to sound crazy, but I'm the man who's going to marry Janice and be the father of your grandchildren."

Gus Crowley brought his left fist into Peter's right eye. There was a crack. Peter staggered. Gus shouted for Janice to run inside and lock the door. Peter said, "No, Janice! Stay with me!" The cop hit him again and a tooth snapped out of his mouth, root and all. Peter hit the lawn as Gus's boot broke into his ribs.

He saw the face of his father-in-law upside down and filled with hatred.

He heard his mother shouting as Dr. Terry rushed at Gus. The pain drained away as he slipped out of the world.

# THIRTY-ONE

Dr. Terry Canyon hurled himself at Gus Crowley and they hit the ground hard. The cop was swinging but Terry was six inches taller, fifty pounds heavier, and had the advantage of surprise. He rolled Gus over and sat on his lower back, pinned one arm behind him, and leaned into his ear. "I'm a doctor. That boy is my patient. The woman is his mother. You need to calm the fuck down."

Joanne Wyatt was cradling the head of her unconscious son and pressing a kerchief to a wound above his right eye. She ordered Wendy DeVille to go into the house and call an ambulance. "Don't knock, go right inside!"

Wendy went in and came face-to-face with a frightened little girl. Wendy smiled and asked if she could please use the telephone. The girl pointed. Wendy dialed for an ambulance and asked the little girl for the address of the house.

"My daddy is a police officer," the little girl said when Wendy hung up. "He can arrest you."

"Oh, he won't want to do that, honey," Wendy said. "This is

all a mix-up. That boy outside made a mistake. He was looking for someone."

"Who was he looking for?"

Wendy wanted to get outside, but she knew she needed to reassure the little girl. She said, "He's looking for a girl named Janice. Janice Crowley." Wendy whispered, "He might have made her up. He's a little silly."

The little girl said, "I'm Janice Crowley."

Wendy pulled back. She was a mother on a mission, but hearing this little girl announce herself as the wife Peter claimed he had lost lifted her into the anti-logic of a dream. Wendy still knew what she had to do, but she no longer knew what to believe.

Peter's mother was speaking to him. She repeated his name. She told him she was right there and he was going to be okay. His lips were bloody and beginning to swell, but his mouth was moving. She leaned in. He said, "Janice? Honey—how did the surgery go? What did the doctor say?"

She said his name again but he was somewhere else. He whispered, "You won't believe the dream I had . . ."

Gus Crowley was shaking but steady as the boy was loaded into the rescue unit. Terry Canyon stood next to the cop, ready to tackle him again if he bolted toward Peter. Two police cars pulled up and the officers came to Gus and conferred with him in low voices. Peter's mother was giving instructions to the ambulance team and glaring back at Gus. Little Janice looked out from inside the screen door.

Wendy was down on her knees in the grass, searching. She found Peter's front tooth and wiped it on her shirt. She wrapped it in a Kleenex and pressed it into Joanne's hand. She said, "The root is still attached. They might be able to save it."

Joanne rode to the emergency room in the ambulance with Peter. She held his hand and spoke to him the whole way.

Dr. Terry followed in the Wyatts' car. Wendy followed Terry in her son's Charger. She felt there was something wrong with the undercarriage.

At the hospital Wendy had to sit in the waiting room while Mrs. Wyatt and Dr. Terry conferred with the nurses. She tried calling home to tell the boys where she was, but no one answered. Her kids never answered the phone. After a full hour Dr. Terry came out and sat next to her. He gave her a reassuring smile.

"Looks like a subdural hematoma, bleeding on the brain. Concussion. His eye will be okay, I think. They put the tooth back in; we'll see if it stays. Not too much worse than a football injury."

His eyes didn't look as optimistic as his smile.

Wendy said, "That little girl was named Janice Crowley. Like Peter said. About his wife?"

Dr. Terry stared straight ahead. "You can find any name in the phone book."

"The dad, the cop, Gus. The town. The house. Everything was like Peter said."

Dr. Terry mumbled, "More things in heaven and earth."

Wendy didn't know what that meant, but it seemed to be intended to kill the conversation.

She finally asked him, "You work with teenagers all the time?"

"Pretty much."

"You figure them out yet?"

He sighed. "You have three boys." Dr. Terry looked straight at Wendy with his striking blue eyes and told her, "I'm certain you know more about the subject than I ever will. There's no substitute for field experience."

"What do you think is really wrong with Peter? Before tonight."

Dr. Terry said softly, "He made a mistake nearly all of us make. He thought he could control how his life would go."

Wendy DeVille and Terry Canyon sat together for another two hours, drinking vending-machine coffee and considering the mysteries.

# THIRTY-TWO

> Yet when we came back, late, from the Hyacinth garden,
> Your arms full, and your hair wet, I could not
> Speak, and my eyes failed, I was neither
> Living nor dead, and I knew nothing
>
> —T. S. Eliot, *The Waste Land*

Peter's mother kneeled by the hospital bed holding the hand of her unconscious son. She spoke into his ear. "You don't have to tell them who you really are. You don't need to say what you're thinking, ever. Keep in your heart what belongs to your heart. Blend in."

Peter's father came into the room.

He looked at his wife bent over her son. He said, "One prediction of Peter's will not come true. That man Gus Crowley will never become chief of police here or anywhere. I very much doubt he'll keep his job. I know some higher-ups in the Long Island judiciary."

A nurse appeared. She asked how our boy was doing. The mother flinched at her calling him that. Peter was her boy.

The nurse lifted one of Peter's eyelids and shined a light. His pupil contracted. His breathing was even. She left. The parents waited.

After an hour the boy lifted his head. He said, "Hey?"

His parents drew close. "How you feeling, Pete?" his father asked.

"What's going on?"

"We're in the hospital," his mother said. "On Long Island."

The boy seemed baffled. "Why are we in a hospital?"

"You got in a fight, son," his father said. "Do you remember?"

"I got in a fight? Who with?"

The nurse returned and said, "Hello, Peter. My name is Claudia. You're in the hospital. How do you feel?"

"Okay . . . ?"

The nurse asked Peter to count backward from twenty to one. He did. She asked him to recite the alphabet, skipping every other letter. He did that too. She asked for his full name and the names of his parents. When he got those right, she said, "Very good. No indication of brain damage."

Peter said, "But you don't know how smart I was before."

A heartbeat passed before everyone laughed. The nurse asked the date and Peter said, "April twelfth, 1970."

The nurse registered no concern but asked him again, and he repeated, "April twelfth, 1970."

The father could not contain himself. He said, "It's June fifth, Peter."

Peter said, "No, no. I have a paper due April fourteenth. It's not June, Dad."

His mother put her hand on her husband's arm. She said to the boy, "Peter, what's the last thing you remember?"

"Last night we watched *Bonanza* and then I went up to bed. We had corn chowder for dinner. Dad was talking about maybe us driving to Vermont next weekend to see Sally."

The parents looked at each other. Peter was describing the night before the delusion began.

When the nurse left, his parents asked a dozen questions about the events of the previous seven weeks. Peter told them he remembered none of it. When they talked about his being an old man from 2020, he assured them he was fifteen and knew very well it was 1970.

A doctor came in to do some tests, and the parents went out into the corridor. Howard said, "Joanne, we have our boy back."

The mother said it did seem that way.

Barry DeVille got his car back, and Wendy saw to it that he didn't press charges. Pressing charges wasn't really Barry's way anyhow. Wendy made sure he didn't exact personal vengeance either.

When Peter heard about the activities of his lost month, starting with stripping naked in front of the class, he said he never wanted to go back to West Bethlehem Veterans Memorial High School again. That was a relief to Moe Mosspaw, who was able to keep a lid on the story of Peter stealing a car and menacing a little girl on Long Island and being beaten unconscious by her police detective father. Mosspaw arranged for Peter to go to summer sessions in a neighboring town. In the autumn he would take up tenth grade at his father's old prep school in New Hampshire. His mother noted with approval that the school was close to Dartmouth. Perhaps Peter would go there for college.

The boy had one more session with Dr. Terry Canyon, who found a very different Peter Wyatt, truculent and sullen.

"You don't remember any of our talks, Pete?" the psychiatrist asked. The boy shook his head and looked at the door like he was planning to run for it.

"How you feeling about leaving your school?"

"Good," Peter said. "I don't want to see any of those idiots again ever."

"Not John North? Not Rick DeVille?"

"Rick DeVille's a fucking creep. I told you, I don't remember anything about playing music with him or his criminal brothers, and I don't want to remember. I just want to forget everything you people say happened to me."

Dr. Terry didn't argue. He kept looking for some indication that the articulate old man he knew was alive in there somewhere, but there was no sign of him. He said, "You're embarrassed about the whole naked in algebra thing, huh?"

The boy made an anguished face and the doctor said, "Peter, I'm going to tell you something that will sound unbelievable to a teenager but is absolutely true. There is very little in this life to be embarrassed about, because—get this—nobody outside your family spends much time thinking about you. You can shave your head, cover your bare butt in peanut butter, and walk into midnight mass with a bullfrog hanging from your dick and everybody will laugh and point and, yes, they will bring it up when they see you, but they won't really think about it too much. The big secret is, most people you meet hardly ever think about you, good or bad, because most people don't care. Now, the first time you realize this it's a disappointment. But believe me, once it sinks in it's a liberation."

Dr. Terry couldn't tell if Peter took any comfort from this. When their hour was up Peter hurried out of the room without making eye contact or saying goodbye. His parents were more grateful and expressed it, but they too were anxious to put the strange visit from Future Peter and the sessions with Dr. Terry behind them.

# THIRTY-THREE

Vice Principal Alice Lockwood did not expressly commend Moe Mosspaw for how he finessed the quiet departure of Peter Wyatt from West Bethlehem Veterans Memorial High School, but one day during finals she said to him in the teachers' lounge, "I'm so glad we put that business with the judge's son to rest without any more hoopla," which in Moe's world was the equivalent of a slap on the back and a free gift certificate to the all-you-can-eat buffet. Moe had a big summer planned, working at the A&P, coaching a CYO softball team, and helping out as a camp counselor on Sundays. Moe Mosspaw did a lot of good for a lot of people and expected no credit, which is what he got.

As soon as summer vacation began, Lou Pitano started officially representing the musical career of Daphne Burrows, who had a regional hit with "Afternoon Delight." For a while Daphne made personal appearances backed up by Ricky and Rocky DeVille, but after Rocky caught her having sex with his big brother, Barry, the group disbanded. Daphne moved to Boston, where she found better musicians and left Lou Pitano for a professional and personal relationship with the manager of the J. Geils Band. A few years later a cover of "Afternoon Delight" by the Starland Vocal Band became a national hit. Daphne earned nine hundred thousand dollars from the publishing.

Motorcycle psychiatrist Terry Canyon came to believe that the strange case of Peter Wyatt was fate's way of leading him to the great love of his life, Wendy DeVille. From the moment they saw each other, he believed they were meant to be together.

Wendy, with her broken beauty and maternal aura, brought out his inner shaman. On a vision quest in a sweat lodge in New Mexico that Christmas he intuited that their future descendants had reached back through time to push Terry and Wendy together through the agency of Peter Wyatt.

At first Wendy was cautious about Terry's advances, but he could get through to her son Ricky in a way no one else ever had. Ricky opened up to Terry while they rebuilt old engines. Terry had a gift for talking with all three of her boys that she had never seen before. He passed through all their defenses. He made her believe that her long run of bad luck had turned around.

At the end of August 1970, two weeks before Peter left for prep school, his parents celebrated their wedding anniversary. They said they didn't want to make a big deal about it, but both of Peter's older sisters came home for the weekend, Cathy pregnant with the first grandchild and Sally home from Vermont. Cathy's husband couldn't make the trip and Sally had broken up with her boyfriend, so it was one of the very rare occasions when Howard and Joanne Wyatt and their three children were all together with no one else, just the original five.

Cathy and Sally knew only the outlines of their little brother's scandal. They picked up the signals from their parents to not pry or tease. Peter had been through something serious enough that he was heading to boarding school. They were relieved that he didn't seem any different at all.

The Saturday of the anniversary weekend was hot and sunny, and the five Wyatts piled into the station wagon and went to Misquamicut Beach on the southern coast of the state. They got there at three, when most of the traffic was heading the other way, and all five of them went into the ocean. The waves were big, and the incline into the sea was gradual up to waist level and then took a quick drop. The family splashed one another and rode the surf and let the waves carry them to shore. They stayed in until the sun was descending and an invasion of seagulls took occupation of the sand.

They rinsed the salt off at outdoor showers and rolled up to Captain Dick's, a seafood restaurant they had visited regularly when the children were small. In the dirt parking lot, Joanne saw Terry Canyon coming out of the restaurant carrying a white take-out bag and two milkshakes. She nudged her husband just in time to see the doctor's companion come up next to him. It took her a moment to recognize Wendy DeVille. Wendy and Terry looked like teenagers on a date.

Dr. Terry spotted the Wyatts and pointed and waved. Wendy DeVille smiled carefully.

"Hey! It's the clan!" Terry cried. "Don't tell me these are the mysterious Wyatt sisters!"

The judge nodded and said hello. He introduced his daughters to Dr. Terry. There was a moment when he couldn't think of Wendy's name, but Joanne filled in for him.

"Wendy," she said. "How did you get this Bostonian so far south?"

Mrs. DeVille said she was introducing Terry to the pleasures of the Ocean State.

Dr. Terry fixed on the boy. “Pete!” he said. “How ya doin’, man? Summer treating you good?”

The boy shifted awkwardly. “Pretty good,” he said. He didn’t make eye contact with the doctor.

The suntanned couple began to walk toward the doctor’s motorcycle when Dr. Terry stopped. He felt for his wallet in his back pocket, took it out, and turned back to the Wyatts.

“Hey, Peter,” he said. “Grab you for a minute?”

Peter’s mother nodded for him to approach the psychiatrist. The doctor moved close to the boy and turned his face to speak to him privately. He opened his wallet and took out two concert tickets. He passed them to Peter.

“The Beatles are coming to Boston,” Dr. Terry said. Peter looked at the tickets. “Harvard Stadium on Labor Day weekend. I got two pair. I want you to go with Wendy and me.”

Peter was nervous. He said, “I can’t take these.”

“Sure you can. Shit, man. It’s the Beatles! First tour in four years. I got them for Rocky and Ricky, but it turns out they hate the Beatles. Of course they do. Maybe you could ask Amy Blessen to be your date.”

Peter shook. “What did I tell you about Amy Blessen?”

“That she’s a cool girl. You asked her out once, you know. In May.”

Peter was shocked. “I did? What did she say?”

“You invited her to go see James Taylor at Brown and she said yes, but then it turned out it was an afternoon show and she had a game. But she was definitely encouraging.” Peter was anxious. Dr. Terry said, "Hey, Pete. You're not even going to the same school anymore. Ask her!"

Peter nodded. Dr. Terry punched him lightly on the shoulder and waved goodbye to the Wyatts with a big smile.

"Who are those people, Dad?" Cathy asked as they passed through the restaurant doors.

"She lives over in Buttongreen," the father said. "He's a psychiatrist from Harvard."

The family took a table by the window and ordered chowder and lemonade and fisherman's platters overflowing with shrimp, clams, scallops, fried sole, and chips. Joanne watched to see if Peter would object to the grease and batter, but he dug in with enthusiasm.

She was sleepy from being in the sun and from stepping out of the heat into the air-conditioning. She felt outside herself. She watched her husband and children as if she were looking at an old movie. All three kids had grown up beautiful, with long legs and arms, tanned skin, and sun-streaked hair. She had made these children, but they weren't hers any longer. They were their own.

She watched Peter and his sisters chattering and joking and considered their living long into the future without her. Someday they would be here together and she would be gone. Her husband would be gone. The kids would live someplace their parents could never enter. It was the country Peter had visited, reported back from, and—she hoped—returned to safely. She surprised herself by feeling jealous. This was her family. She had made them and devoted her life to them, but they would keep on being a family when she was gone.

Peter looked away from his sisters and returned her gaze. She studied his face for any sign of the displaced sixty-five-year-old, but then Sally swiped one of his french fries and he yipped at her, and Joanne knew he was her fifteen-year-old boy.

"Our children pass into another life," she thought, "where they will be secure and easeful, into which we can never go."

Peter said, "Are you still with us, Mom?"

"I'm right here," she said.

The boy looked at her like he knew her thoughts. He said, "Then we are all where we're meant to be."